Dr. Jekyll and Mr. Seek

The Strange Case Continues

ANTHONY O'NEILL

Skyhorse Publishing
A Herman Graf book

First Skyhorse edition 2018
First published 2017 by Black & White Publishing Ltd

Skyhorse Publishing books may be purchased in bulk at special discounts for sales promotion, corporate gifts, fund-raising, or educational purposes. Special editions can also be created to specifications. For details, contact the Special Sales Department, Skyhorse Publishing, 307 West 36th Street, 11th Floor, New York, NY 10018 or info@skyhorsepublishing.com.

Skyhorse® and Skyhorse Publishing® are registered trademarks of Skyhorse Publishing, Inc.®, a Delaware corporation.

Visit our website at www.skyhorsepublishing.com.

10 9 8 7 6 5 4 3 2 1

Library of Congress Cataloging-in-Publication Data is available on file.

Cover design by Thomas Ross
Cover illustration credit: Shutterstock

Print ISBN: 978-1-5107-3781-5
Ebook ISBN: 978-1-5107-3785-3

Printed in the United States of America

This book is dedicated to the memory of
EILEEN ELIZABETH O'NEILL,
who walked the streets of Melbourne
looking for Dr. Jekyll and Mr. Hyde.

'If he be Mr. Hyde, I shall be Mr. Seek.'

Gabriel Utterson in Robert Louis Stevenson's
The Strange Case of Dr. Jekyll and Mr. Hyde

A Misted Window

A SULPHUROUS YELLOW FOG, so thick it muffled the chimes of the Sunday church bells, had fastened overnight to London and refused to be dislodged by even the stiffest of breezes. It smothered domes and spires, blurred chimneys and gables, smudged walls and windows, and altogether turned the city into an immense spectral museum, through which even the most audacious traveller proceeded warily, never certain of what strange sights might lurk in the next chamber.

Mr. Gabriel Utterson, the bald and birdlike lawyer, and his distant kinsman Mr. Richard Enfield, the dashing man about town, were more than familiar with London fogs, having conducted their Sunday walks together for nearly eighteen years. Yet it is by no means certain that, were it not for the density of this particular fog on this particular day, they would have found themselves in a by-street of peculiar infamy.

'Well,' said Enfield, after a moment's hesitation, 'I should not need to tell you where the hand of fate has guided us.'

'I know the street well enough,' replied Utterson.

'A certain building—yes, I see it now. A place as disagreeable as the man who emerged from it.'

'He has not emerged from it for some time now. Nor from any other building, I wager.'

'And yet, I can still see his face,' mused Enfield, 'as if it were yesterday.'

Both men were staring across the street, where not far from the corner was a windowless building with a frowning gable and a dark, blistered door. And both men remembered, with remarkable immediacy, the hideous little man called Hyde who had scuttled out of that door, and slithered into the night, and enacted crimes so evil that they still had the power to chill the blood, even when viewed through the misted window of memory.

'How long has it been now?' asked Enfield.

'Nearly seven years,' his companion replied.

'Seven years? Since he trampled over that poor girl? And murdered Sir Danvers Carew?'

'And took his own life, in those very dissecting rooms.'

'Seven years . . .' said Enfield, staring fixedly at the place. 'Then it is also seven years,' he went on, 'since Jekyll disappeared?'

'Quite so.'

'Meaning that you, being Jekyll's lawyer and sole beneficiary, will shortly be taking possession of his estate?'

'Within two weeks, in fact.'

'Including all his property?'

'As Jekyll himself directed.'

Enfield nodded slowly, still looking across the street. 'Then how, may I ask, are you inclined to deal with it?'

'With the dissecting rooms?' Utterson asked. 'I intend to sell them as soon as possible, for they hold no value to me—and little to anyone else, I fancy.'

The younger man nodded. 'There is nothing good to be said for them,' he said. 'So let us hope they are soon demolished, and quickly forgotten.'

'Quite right,' said Utterson.

But both men knew that this was only half the story, for the dissecting rooms were connected at their rear to another, more presentable, building, which in turn faced onto another, more presentable, street. And it was to inspect the front of this other residence that the two men now progressed, as if by some tacit agreement, down to the corner and across the square.

'We enjoyed some splendid dinners with Jekyll there,' said Enfield, looking back.

'We did indeed.'

'Henry was an exceptional host.'

'He was.'

'He had exquisite taste in most things.'

'That, too, cannot be denied.'

Enfield nodded. 'Are you intending to sell his home as well?'

'No, I cannot bear to do so,' said Utterson. 'Of all the houses in London, it has always been my favourite. I would hate to relinquish it now.'

'I doubt Henry would want you to,' Enfield said.

'I doubt it, too.'

The two men regarded the handsome façade, with its gleaming windows, polished bricks and mullioned door, for close to a minute.

'So what, indeed, are your plans for the place?'

'Well,' said Utterson, shifting, 'I might yet make some use of it, you know.'

'Indeed?'

'It would be a pity to let it go empty.'

'I suppose so.'

Enfield's curiosity sounded innocent enough, but Utterson had a sense he was skirting around something—some disquieting revelation, perhaps. So the two men stood stiffly for a while, and finally the younger one sighed.

'You know, I must tell you something, dear friend. And not with any relish, I'm bound.'

'Oh?'

'Something I overheard at my club. A conversation about the fate of Jekyll, and your part in the whole business.'

'My part, you say?'

'It was some months ago now, and to this day I've not cared to mention it. But as I'm to leave town tomorrow, and as you're about to take over the estate, it might be best that you became aware of some of the mutterings that are abroad.'

'Mutterings?' Utterson said, frowning. 'And what indeed are these mutterings?'

'No'—Enfield appeared to change his mind—'I shan't repeat it. Claptrap, the lot of it. But you should brace yourself, dear friend, lest any of the slander reaches your ears.'

Utterson did not say it, but some of the slander—to the effect that he had played some sinister role in Jekyll's disappearance, even rewritten the doctor's will in his own favour—had already reached his ears. And while he never enjoyed hearing such calumnies, he could scarcely help being curious about them.

'Do tell, at least, what gave rise to such talk.'

'There was a new member at my club,' Enfield said, 'who proved especially curious about Jekyll. I cannot remember his name, and I've not encountered him since.'

'He gave no reason for asking such questions?'

'Well, he had good reason after the sordid death of that other Jekyll—Thomas Jekyll, Henry's brother.'

'A half-brother,' said Utterson. 'Henry mentioned him once, without any affection.'

'Still, the particulars of his demise appeared in *The Times*, together with a reference to Henry's previous disappearance— you must remember?'

'I remember. And this prompted the stranger to enquire about me?'

'Chiefly about Henry, but your name surfaced now and then. Nonsense, I say. Nonsense, the lot of it.'

Enfield did not elaborate, and Utterson decided he did not really care to pry—not on this day, in any event. Somewhere a hurdy-gurdy player was cranking out carnival tunes; a dog was yapping furiously; someone was laughing like a demon. The two men, unsettled, were about to move on when Enfield leaned forward.

'I say,' he said, squinting into the mist, 'is that smoke, rising from Jekyll's chimney?'

Utterson, adjusting his spectacles, saw a stain of dark smoke curling into the fog.

'Seems so,' he said, shrugging. 'The housekeeper, no doubt. I've engaged one to maintain the home, in the absence of any other staff.'

'Lives in the place, does she?'

'No, but she is in possession of a key, and works when she pleases.'

'On a Sunday?'

'It makes sense, as she has duties elsewhere.'

In truth Utterson was further unsettled by the sight, but the accumulation of sour memories and sensations, so unsuited to the humour of their weekly stroll, left him ill-equipped for more unpleasantness. So he changed the subject.

'In any case,' he said, 'this is not getting us any closer to our destination.'

'I suppose not,' said Enfield—though in truth the two men, in all their years of ambling, had never really had a precise destination.

For all that, when they parted, after enjoying a lark pie and coffee at Pagani's, it was with a great deal of warmth and not a little sadness. Enfield passed across the key to his apartment, so that his kinsman might inspect the place in his absence, then the two men shook hands vigorously before going their separate ways, Utterson heading solemnly for south London and Enfield moving at a clip towards Piccadilly—neither man suspecting that one of them would shortly be dead.

A Divided Self

T HE NEXT DAY Utterson was at his desk, poring over some financial documents, when his head clerk, Mr. Guest, appeared at the door.

'A flighty woman in the entrance hall. In housemaid flannels. She insists she is in your employ, sir.'

'Did she give a name?'

'Calls herself Miss Finnegan.' Guest sniffed. 'Irish, I believe.'

'Please, Mr. Guest, send her in.'

In normal circumstances Utterson might have been grateful for the distraction. After twenty-five years of conveyancing, estate management, wills and probate, he sighed with every heave of the pen. His eyesight was weakening, his tolerance of triviality was strained, and there were times when he could not prevent his mind from wandering helplessly. So any unexpected visit, any opportunity to engage in conversation, would on most days have been a welcome diversion. But the memory of Jekyll's smoking chimney had pumped a pall over his imagination all night, and he was loath to consider any fresh complications.

'Don't mean to disturb you, sir,' said the housemaid, shuffling through the door, 'but I reckoned it best that I come here in person.'

'Please, Miss Finnegan, take a seat.'

'Oh, that's orright, sir, don't you worry about me, I ain't got much to say, only what's happened at the Jekyll place just now.'

'At the Jekyll . . .?' Utterson frowned. 'And what indeed has happened?'

'I went there this mornin', sir, and I tried to open the front door with that key you gave me, sir, and as soon as I tried . . . as soon as I tried'—she spluttered; a persistent cough—'a gentleman opened the door . . . a gentleman, no, I could not call him that . . . a brute he was, a mean-faced brute with a pug-dog's face, and he told me to be on my way, for I had no business there.'

'And who was this man, to order you about that way?'

'He did not name 'isself, sir, but I think he was a butler.'

'A butler? You say the man was a butler?'

'I believe so, sir, by the way he was decked out.'

Utterson's pulse was quickening. 'Did he happen to give you the name of his employer?'

'No, sir—just told me to clear off, and snarled at me like a dog.'

'Then tell me, Miss Finnegan, were you at the Jekyll home yesterday?'

'Why no, sir, I was at Mr. Cremorne's.'

'So you did not light a fire?'

'No, sir, not on a Sunday.'

'Then the house might have been occupied for days, do you think?'

'I s'pose so, sir—why? What are you to do?'

As a lawyer Utterson was disposed to seek redress through writs and applications, through the power of pen and oratory.

He was a man of the most rigid formality, not one given to rash actions. But now, presented with this very personal infraction—a threat to his very hopes and dreams—he found himself getting indignantly to his feet.

'I shall sort this out,' he said, 'that's what I shall do.' He reached for his hat and cane. 'And not a minute too soon, by the sounds of it.'

Outside, the lurid veins of a winter sunset suffused the air with sanguinary tints. The lamplighters in their fustian jackets were just commencing their rounds. The streets were alive with shouts and shrieks, grinding wheels and huffing horses. But Utterson, launching himself into a cab, saw and heard none of it. He did not even feel the sting of the sub-arctic wind. He was warmed by his own pounding pulse, and his head was swirling with speculations.

Utterson's great secret—so private that he had not fully admitted it to anyone, not even to Enfield—was that he planned to move into the Jekyll home once it came legally into his possession, and give over his old one, the Gaunt Street address where he had resided for nearly twenty years, to a widow by the name of Nora Spratling.

Bryant was her name when she trampled over young men's hearts. Utterson, a carefree law student at the time, was one of those crushed; his close friend Hastie Lanyon was another; while Henry Jekyll, for a long time seemingly Nora's principal love, had somehow escaped devastation. But in the end she had settled on a much senior businessman—a speculator by the name of Albert Spratling—whose chief attraction, it seemed to his rivals, was a fortune of mysterious provenance.

Still, it had been, for much longer than it deserved to be, the happiest of unions. The couple settled into Spratling's Cornwall estate where they were renowned for their hunts, banquets and masquerades (some of them said to be attended by figures of great renown, such as the Duke of Marlborough). But eventually the past caught up with the old speculator (clubbed to death during a spell in debtors' prison), leaving Nora with scant sympathy from a battalion of creditors.

In desperation she turned for legal counsel to Gabriel Utterson, the man who most adored her; and she had relocated to London both to settle her titanic debts and to be closer to the doctors treating her dumbstruck son. She was living now in a beetle-infested terrace house in the back streets of Shepherd's Bush . . . and to Utterson, at least, she seemed more fetching than ever. So of course he found the idea irresistible: Nora Bryant installed in his old abode, like a parrot in a cage, while he occupied the home of her one true love, Dr. Henry Jekyll. The full permutations were too dizzying to contemplate.

Presently he arrived at the familiar square, where a high wind was shrieking through the trees. Setting his jaw, he mounted Jekyll's steps, seized the sizable doorknocker and rapped out a military drumroll. Then, there being no immediate response, he thumped on the wood with his lion-headed cane.

Finally there was a shifting of bolts and a twisting of knobs as the door, as thick as a bank vault's, swung back to reveal a bull-like man in a black surcoat. The man surveyed Utterson over a twisted nose but said nothing.

'And who,' demanded the lawyer, 'are you?'

The man did not reply.

'I asked your name, sir—kindly tell me your name.'

'My name,' drawled the man, 'is Baxter.'

'And what are you doing here?'

'I am a butler.'

Utterson had half a mind to push his way past, but the man was the size of the Minotaur. 'A butler for whom? You must know these are not your premises, and you have no—'

But the butler, to Utterson's astonishment, merely closed the door.

Utterson stood on the doorstep for half a minute, appalled by the insolence. Then he remembered that he had a key—of course he did—and every right to use it. So he extracted it from his pocket and inserted it in the lock. But as hard as he tried the key would not connect. The lock had been replaced.

Utterson backed onto the pavement and looked up. A man's shadow caressed the curtains and the light dimmed.

Someone had *taken possession* of the Jekyll home. Someone had *changed the locks*. It was an outrage; a brazen crime. And Utterson could not just walk away from it. He mounted the steps and pounded and hammered afresh. He called for attention. Windows across the square flew up, shutters flew open. Finally a glow appeared at the fanlight and the door creaked open again.

'This will not do, sir,' declared Utterson. '*This will not do.*'

'I must ask you to leave, sir,' snarled the bent-nosed butler. 'Or I shall be forced to summon the police.'

'*You* threaten *me* with the police?'

'My master is unwell—he requires his rest.'

'Your master! Your master, you say? And who in God's name is your master?'

The butler sniffed, as if the question were too asinine to warrant an answer. 'My master, in God's name, is Dr. Henry Jekyll.'

Upon which he slammed the door with such force that the breath was knocked from Utterson's lungs.

The Custodian of Secrets

UTTERSON'S FIRST IMPULSE was to march directly to the nearest police station. But he thought the better of it before even reaching the corner—the local constabulary would surely have changed a good deal in the intervening seven years, and the new PCs could hardly be expected to be familiar with the full complexities of the Jekyll affair.

So he hailed a hansom and headed instead for Scotland Yard, where Francis Newcomen, the policeman originally assigned to the case, now held the post of Detective Inspector. Yet even by this course Utterson was by no means certain of success, owing to a pivotal decision he had made one unforgettable night in March of 18—.

It was on that evening that Mr. Poole, the devoted butler of Dr. Jekyll, had arrived breathless at Utterson's door in Gaunt Street claiming that Mr. Hyde had seized control of the dissecting rooms and was growling orders from behind the laboratory door. And this to Utterson was a most disturbing development, since Jekyll had vowed never more to have dealings with Mr. Hyde, who was wanted for murder among innumerable other atrocities.

So Utterson raced with Poole to the Jekyll home, broke down the door with an axe, and inside found Hyde twitching on the floor, having just consumed a phial of poison. But of the doctor himself there was no sign apart from a couple of freshly written documents: one a revised will, that appeared to name Utterson as his sole beneficiary; the other a bulky confession that the lawyer bundled straightaway into his pocket.

'I would say nothing of this paper,' he said to Poole. 'If your master has fled or is dead, we may at least save his credit.' He glanced at the clock. 'It is now ten; I must go home and read these documents in quiet; but I shall be back before midnight, when we shall send for the police.'

Back home in Gaunt Street Utterson drew the curtains, lit a fire, took up his customary position before the hearth and read, for the very first time, Henry Jekyll's full statement of the case (along with a letter from the late Hastie Lanyon, which by instruction was to be opened only in the event of Jekyll's disappearance).

An hour later he rose, returned his hat to his head, tugged on his gloves, retrieved his cane, and started back for the Jekyll home. But he did not hail a cab; he did not even walk with particular urgency. With a bracing wind needling his face, and the coldness of the pavement prickling his feet through the soles of his shoes, he walked blankly, his brow creased, his eyes distant and his mind spinning like a dervish.

If what he had just read was true—and he had no reason to disbelieve it—then Henry Jekyll, one of his firmest and oldest friends, was now dead on the floor of his own laboratory. Jekyll had not been just a companion of Mr. Hyde's—he *was* Mr. Hyde. He had formulated a potion that transformed his appearance and dismantled his inhibitions, unleashing from within a raging monster. Which meant that the mystery that had confounded Utterson for sixteen months—who was the demonic little man called Hyde, and what was his strange power over Jekyll?—finally had an answer. But it was an answer so shocking that Hastie Lanyon, to whom Jekyll had been compelled to divulge his secret unexpectedly, had withered under its burden and died within days of writing his own statement of the case.

Still, Utterson prided himself on being made of sterner stuff than that. In his life he had endured broken hearts and family tragedies and bouts of youthful self-loathing; by profession he had become acquainted with all species of swindlers, forgers and malefactors; and through it all he had become renowned for his patience and imperturbability. It was not for nothing that he had become a custodian of other men's secrets; and not without reason that Lanyon and Jekyll had identified him as the priest of their extreme unction.

So as he strode across the city that terrible night, with his face set and his stomach clenched, he resolved on absolute circumspection—a species of prudence of which few other men would be capable. He would tell no one the truth—not a soul, not even Enfield. For what good would it do now? What purpose would it serve? The villain Hyde was dead and punished, and his creator along with him. But whereas Hyde would be remembered for nothing but infamy, Jekyll would at least maintain his reputation *post mortem*.

When Poole admitted him back into Jekyll's entrance hall, where a fire was flashing on the panels, Utterson was already warmed by his own chivalry.

'May I ask about the letters?' said Poole.

'Nothing,' clicked Utterson. 'Just some directions for his property and the disbursement of funds.'

'Nothing about Mr. Hyde?'

'Not a word.'

'And no indication . . . no indication that my master might return?'

Utterson was moved by the butler's concern. 'I'm afraid to say, Poole, that the wording of the letter leads me to suspect we shall not be seeing Henry Jekyll again—*ever.*'

And then, after allowing Poole a few moments to collect himself, he added discreetly: 'Though I still think it would be best, don't you, to say nothing about the document? To a soul?' Thereby hinting at something unmentionable, without betraying any indication of its true nature.

'Aye,' said Poole, swallowing his dismay. 'It's best to let such things rest in peace.'

'Very well put, Poole, very well put. It's time for everyone— *all* the victims of this sad affair—to rest in peace.'

And so, for seven whole years, they had.

Presently Utterson, after correcting his course one or two times, arrived at Scotland Yard, finding the building nigh on unrecognisable under scaffolding and builders' drapery. Introducing himself at the front desk, he was directed through a warren of chambers to the detective division, where in the waiting room a solitary lamp was hissing in its bracket. Detective Inspector Newcomen, looking as renovated as the building—for in seven years he had acquired an impressive moustache, muttonchops and purplish pouches under his eyes—greeted him indifferently and ushered him into his room.

'You're lucky to find me here, Mr. Utterson—I'm overdue for dinner with my brood.'

'Oh,' said Utterson, 'you have a family now?'

'A wife and three young 'uns.'

'Then I shan't delay you for long,' Utterson said. 'It's just that a serious matter has arisen, and you seem the best-equipped man to deal with it.'

Installing himself in a seat, he told the inspector of the smoking chimney, Miss Finnegan's curt dismissal and his own visit to the Jekyll home, where he had been turned away by the belligerent butler.

'And not only that,' he went on, 'but the man claimed that his master was Dr. Henry Jekyll.'

'Henry Jekyll, eh?' Newcomen was twining one end of his moustache. 'The same Jekyll who's been missing all these years?'

'For nearly seven years.'

'The one who was the sponsor of Mr. Hyde?'

'That's correct.'

'The one who bequeathed his estate—his property and all his investments—to you?'

'He did.'

'And now he's back in business, is he?'

Utterson baulked. 'Well, whoever the man is, he's an impostor, of course—a swindler of some sort. I don't need to say that.'

'Saw him, did you?'

'No, I was blockaded at the front door, as I explained.'

'So you saw nothing of Dr. Jekyll himself?'

'Of the man claiming to be Jekyll—nothing at all.'

Newcomen considered this awhile and finally released his moustache. 'Then how do you know, Mr. Utterson, that it was *not* Dr. Jekyll?'

'My dear sir,' Utterson said, before finding himself stymied. 'It can't be Jekyll . . . it simply cannot be. It's impossible.'

'Impossible? Why?'

'Why?' Utterson had not expected such scepticism from a detective so familiar with the original case. Sitting forward in his chair, he said, 'Inspector, you will have to believe me. It's been seven years. And I *know* Henry Jekyll—or at least I *did* know him. And I *know* this cannot be Jekyll, for many good reasons. It simply cannot be. The real Jekyll has disappeared. The real Jekyll has . . . *gone*.'

But his voice tightened as he said these words, because of course he could not explain how he knew this for certain. And he sensed, in light of the detestable rumours, that he could not afford to look *too* flustered at the thought of Jekyll's return.

'Then I'll look into it tomorrow,' Newcomen decided. 'I'll make a little visit to the Jekyll residence and have a word with the good doctor.'

'Not the doctor,' Utterson insisted. 'An impostor.'

'As it may be,' sniffed Newcomen. 'As it may be.'

Utterson curbed an impulse to protest further. 'Very well,' he said, pushing himself to his feet with his cane. 'Then I shall hear from you tomorrow, during the course of the day?'

'Very probably.'

But Newcomen was looking distractedly through some papers as he said this, giving no indication, it seemed to a deflated Utterson, that he regarded the matter as anything more than a trifle.

A Malfunctioning Clock

A MAN OF CLOCKWORK precision, Utterson invariably sank into his chainspring mattress with the midnight chimes and within minutes was fast asleep. But on this particular night he lay mummy-like in his blankets for many hours into the morning, puffing clouds of steam into the air, his mind gnawing ravenously on his own indignation.

The victim of a brazen fraud, he knew from his legal experience, is someone who feels uniquely violated. The arrogance of the fraud, the sheer cunning necessary to facilitate it and above all the very *personal* aspect of the deed—these alone were enough to make any victim feverish with rage.

And in Utterson's case it was all compounded by the knowledge that he was hopelessly hobbled by the unwritten pact he had made with Jekyll's legacy. Who would believe him if he told the truth, anyway? A distinguished doctor ingests a foaming potion and transforms into a murderous troglodyte? And then reverts to the person of the distinguished doctor? Until he loses all control of the process and transmogrifies willy-nilly? It was unscientific balderdash, the stuff of fever dreams and sensation novels. No, Utterson could never espouse such notions.

He would have to rely on the impostor's being expeditiously weeded out by some other means, which was surely just a matter of time.

When the bells sounded four o'clock and the chimney sweepers started scrabbling across the roofs, Utterson decided to quell his nerves with a soothing vintage. In his nightshirt he crept down the stairs and by candlelight unlocked the wine cellar, where he removed from its roost his finest Bordeaux.

On his way back across the vault, however, he stepped on a rat and lost hold of the bottle, which smashed noisily across the stones.

'Damnation!' he hissed, and the candle flame flared.

Picking his way gingerly over the shattered glass—he was still in his bedsocks—he selected another, altogether inferior, vintage and was locking the door when he noticed Poole brandishing a lamp.

'Something amiss, sir?'

'It's nothing, Poole—I dropped a bottle.'

'Would sir like it cleared away?'

'In the morning, of course.'

'Then you'll need to leave behind the key to the cellar.'

'I'll do that, Poole.'

'And do you wish me to lay down poison for the rats while I'm there?'

'Yes, of course.'

'Then I'll need some money from sundry expenses, sir.'

'In the morning, Poole—I'll leave you some cash in the morning.'

'Very well,' the butler said. 'Pleasant dreams, sir.'

'And to you, Mr. Poole—pleasant dreams.'

But Utterson did not miss the implied disapproval—the same air of sufferance Poole had been cultivating ever since he moved into Gaunt Street. Clearly the old butler, though prudent enough never to voice his displeasure openly, pined for the days when he presided over the home of Dr. Jekyll, fussed over the doctor's lavish dinners, and played curator to his considerable cellar (which unlike Utterson's was never locked). In Utterson's house he had been burdened with the roles of butler, footman, cook and housemaid, and further had to contend with airless little rooms that were the very antithesis of what he had patrolled in the Jekyll home. (Even Utterson's efforts to make his place more agreeable—in preparation for Nora's arrival he had introduced brocaded wallpaper, fluted lampshades and a fireplace so immense it resembled the proscenium at the Adelphi—seemed only to accentuate its ugliness.)

In any case—and despite Poole's unconvincing wishes—the wine did little to abet Utterson's sleep; he stared through the window at the gaslights of the heavens; he saw two shooting stars; when he dreamed it was only of the swollen and blistered dissecting rooms' door; and in the morning he felt so bleary-eyed that he pointedly avoided looking at himself in the mirror. He shaved, breakfasted and headed off to work with all the enthusiasm of a soldier marching into a cannonade.

He had barely alighted from his cab when he heard a voice.

'Utterson, dear fellow! Capital news, eh?'

Sir Palfrey Bramble, the intrepid explorer, was trundling up Bedford Row in a hackney coach.

'News?' Utterson called.

'About Henry Jekyll's return,' exclaimed Sir Palfrey, before adding, with all the candour of a man who has spent thirty years among savages and jungle beasts, 'Not so good for you though, what?'

He was quickly out of range, though, leaving Utterson confounded. Where had Bramble learned the news? Why had he not seen fit to question it? Why, indeed, did he think it was 'capital'? Utterson ended up so distracted that he spent much of the morning attending to his own mistakes—misspellings in his briefs, ink stains on his ledger.

And still nothing from Inspector Newcomen. Nor did his regular excursions to the front desk, seeking any fresh delivery of mail, yield any satisfaction. In the afternoon he considered making a lightning trip home—perhaps Newcomen had sent a cable there—or even heading directly to Scotland Yard. But he knew he could not afford to look too eager or presumptuous.

So he endured the day at Bedford Row, his tension preventing him from falling asleep; and when the clocks sounded seven o'clock he hurtled down the stairs and rattled home in a cab, his hand clenched so tightly around his cane that he almost snapped it in half.

In Gaunt Street Poole was waiting with the afternoon mail. 'A special delivery, sir.'

Utterson took it greedily and sidled into his parlour, where he tore open the envelope and held the letter under the nearest lamp.

But the note—it was written in violet ink—was not from Inspector Newcomen at all. In fact, to Utterson's irritation, it purported to be from Jekyll himself.

His eyes raced furiously across the words:

My dear Utterson—,

I trust you will forgive me for the curt reception you received last evening from my butler, Mr. Baxter, and the discourteous manner in which you were turned away from my door. But my faith in your good nature renders me confident that you will understand there is much with which I am still re-acquainting myself, and the conduct of my servants, not to mention the sensitivities of my friends, have to this point ranked low among my priorities.

Nonetheless you can rest assured that you remain my firmest friend and (I dearly hope) my most reliable ally in my time of need. I bid you therefore to be tolerant of my many shortcomings, and as generous as always with your assistance, should I call upon you at any time.

To introduce myself back into society I shall be hosting a dinner, to commence at eight o'clock on Saturday evening. I acknowledge that this comes at rather short notice; but there is no one, dear Utterson, whose presence at the meal is more important to me than your own.

Your everlasting friend,
HENRY JEKYLL

Your everlasting friend . . . Utterson was still staring at the words, appalled by the man's gall, when he became aware of Poole peering over his shoulder. Swiftly he lowered the letter and buried it in his pocket.

'Forgive me, sir,' said the butler, straightening.

'It's nothing,' said Utterson. 'Nothing.'

Poole, however, seemed reluctant to retreat. 'S-sir,' he said, 'may I ask?'

'Ask what?'

'Was that . . . was that by some chance a letter from Dr. Jekyll?'

Utterson frowned. 'What the devil makes you think that?'

'Oh, I know it seems foolish, sir, but it looked so much like his writing—right there on the envelope, I mean. And I knew his hand so well, after all.'

'Then you're mistaken, Poole, very much mistaken. This is not a letter from Jekyll—how could it be?'

'But it looks so much like his writing, as I say.'

'Mr. Poole, you're mistaken. It's just a letter, from a client of mine. A . . .' But for a terrible moment Utterson could think of no suitable profession. 'A . . . a banker of some sort.'

And he glared at the butler so fiercely that Poole twitched and swallowed like a nervous hound. 'I'm very sorry, sir . . . I don't know what I was thinking.'

'Nor do I, Poole. Nor do I.'

Minutes later Utterson lit a fire in his hearth and consigned the letter to the flames. But he did not destroy the envelope itself. He held it tightly in his hand all through the night, like a suicide note, even in those few minutes when his mind cooled sufficiently to permit him some sleep.

The Shadow on the Curtains

A T HIS OFFICE in the morning Utterson laid out the impostor's envelope next to one addressed years earlier by the genuine Henry Jekyll, then summoned to his desk Mr. Guest. It had been his head clerk, something of a student of handwriting, who many years earlier had noticed the marked similarity between the scripts of Dr. Jekyll and Mr. Hyde.

'Look closely at this handwriting,' Utterson said to him now, sliding across the authentic article, 'and tell me if you recognise it.'

'Why yes, sir, that's Dr. Jekyll's hand—I'd know it anywhere.'

'Particularly distinctive, is it?'

'The doctor had a singular flair for most things. You can see it in the confidence of his curls, and the firmness of his strokes.'

Utterson grunted. 'Then cast your keen eye over this one,' he said, sliding across the envelope that he had been clutching all night.

Guest studied it for much longer than Utterson expected.

'Well?' the lawyer said.

'Well . . . I'm not sure, sir.'

'It's a plain forgery, is it not?'

'It's difficult to say.'

'What about the curls and strokes—you're not saying they're the same in both samples?'

'Not quite . . . this script lacks the other's confidence—'

'Of course it does.'

'But, if I may say, sir'—Guest still seemed hesitant—'there are many more similarities than differences . . . and it's not uncommon, after all, for a man's writing to evolve with the passage of years.'

'With the passage of years? How do you . . .'

But Utterson stilled his tongue. It struck him that Guest might be indicating that he, like Sir Palfrey Bramble before him, was already acquainted with the news of Jekyll's return. But if so, why had he not mentioned it? Why had he not asked Jekyll's oldest and dearest friend—Utterson himself—if it could possibly be true? Disconcerted, he collected his two envelopes and locked them in a drawer.

'Never mind,' he said. 'It doesn't matter.' Then he rose, buttoning his coat. 'I'm heading out for a while.'

Guest looked surprised. 'What about your nine o'clock appointment with Mr. Spurlock, sir?'

'Spurlock's needs can be adequately served by Mr. Slaughter. Or even by you, for that matter.'

Utterson collected his hat and umbrella—there was a fine rain swirling about—and set forth into the streets. Near Drury Lane he was buffeted by a malodorous drunk; he barely noticed. Near Trafalgar Square an overworked carthorse had collapsed, half-crushing a child; he walked straight past. When he arrived at Scotland Yard he asked to see Detective Inspector Newcomen, half-expecting, even hoping, to hear some sort of excuse—that the inspector had been called out of town or some such thing—but to his alarm he was directed to the detective department. Here he spent fifteen minutes staring blankly at the noticeboards before Newcomen appeared and directed him to his desk.

'I s'pose you're here about the Jekyll business.'

'I am,' said Utterson, already disliking the inspector's tone.

'Hm, well.' Newcomen thrust out his chin. 'I made a visit there yesterday, as I said I would. And I saw this chap you spoke of, the servant fellow Baxter.'

'Ah yes, Mr. Baxter.'

'Says he used to be a boxer. And a sailor. And a circus strongman. Interesting fellow.'

'And what about the master of the house? Did you happen to meet him?'

'Well yes, I met him too. And we had a very revealing chat, as it happens. Spoke about a good deal of things, we did.'

Utterson blinked. 'And you ordered him to vacate the premises immediately, naturally. You warned him he would be arrested otherwise.'

Newcomen sniffed. 'And why would I do that, exactly?'

'Why?' Utterson could scarcely believe the inspector's attitude. 'Because the man is a charlatan, of course!'

'Now see here, Mr. Utterson, that remains to be seen, does it not? His story held water, it seemed to me. And he spoke with a saint's conviction. So I decided to let him be for now.'

'You decided to let him be!'

'Until I have more reason to doubt him, yes. He's going to be collecting affidavits in the next few days, he says, from friends and the like. And once he's done that, and established his credentials, he'll make moves to reclaim his estate.'

'Oh he will, will he?'

'He mentioned you, too. Something about his old lawyer friend being sure to help him out.'

'He mentioned me by name?'

'"That dear fellow Utterson", he said. Has a lot of time for you, the doctor has, even after all these years.'

To Utterson it was increasingly preposterous. 'But really, Inspector, you're not saying you believed him? That you truly believed him?'

'Why would I not?'

Utterson drew a breath. 'Now wait a minute, Inspector. Now that I think of it, you never did meet Dr. Jekyll, did you? I mean the real Dr. Jekyll—you never met him as Jekyll. If memory serves, you only met him when he was . . . I mean to say, you only met Mr. Hyde. After Sir Danvers Carew was murdered, you accompanied me to Hyde's lodgings in Soho. But you never actually met Jekyll in the flesh, did you?'

Newcomen stiffened. 'Maybe not, but I know the doctor's appearance well enough. I was the one who put out his description when he was declared missing.'

'Yes, but you never looked him square in the face, did you? You never shook his hand. Conversed with him. You never knew him as an acquaintance, let alone a friend. So you have no grounds on which to judge, do you, whether this impostor is Jekyll?'

Newcomen grunted. 'And neither do you, Mr. Utterson, if you've not yet seen him, as you fully admit.'

'But I don't *need* to see him,' Utterson insisted. 'I don't need to . . .' But again he trailed off.

'Seems to me, Mr. Utterson,' Newcomen said, stroking his moustache, 'that you would do well to re-introduce yourself to the fellow. He's holding a dinner on Saturday, and inviting all his friends. So why not delay your judgement until then? If he's a charlatan, as you say he is, then I'm sure he'll trip himself up sooner or later. And if he's not, well, at least we won't see an innocent man in chains.'

'An innocent man?' Utterson scoffed. 'In chains? Let me tell you, sir, this fellow . . .'

But he bit his tongue. His emotions were getting the better of him again. So he forced himself to mumble an apology to Newcomen and effected a swift retreat.

But that night, huddled into his greatcoat, he returned to Jekyll's street, the landscape he had watched like a thousand-eyed Argus in the days when he was trying to unravel the mystery of Mr. Hyde. Finding refuge in the door of a barbershop—it used to be a draper's, just as the place next door had been a map-seller's—he waited until he saw a shadow fall across Jekyll's curtains, then marched across the square and pounded on the door.

'Mr. Baxter,' Utterson said, when the butler appeared. 'I trust that you remember me?'

'I do.'

'I've come to speak to your master.'

'My master is absent.'

'Absent, is he?'

'Visiting friends.'

'Balderdash,' said Utterson. 'Your master is upstairs. I saw him moments ago at the bedroom window. Now allow me to speak to him or—'

But again, to Utterson's astonishment, Baxter simply shut the door.

Reeling—for he had been foolish enough to accept the impostor's apology for his butler's insolence—Utterson stepped back onto the pavement and looked up. But the light was no longer burning above.

For a moment he considered returning home and licking his wounds, holding off until the Saturday dinner, exactly as New-comen had suggested. But in the end he retreated only as far as the barbershop door, waiting for some new development.

He was there for perhaps three hours, diving into the shadows whenever a PC or a tradesman strolled past, but he saw nothing untoward until close to two o'clock, when a ragged little man in knee-length trousers and a calico cap came trudging through the square. Utterson did not pay much attention to him at first—the fellow, who was bearing a bulging sack over his shoulder, looked like a common rag-and-bone man—but when the fellow rounded the corner into the by-street Utterson noticed the flash of a key being drawn from his pocket.

Startled, he raced across the square and down the street, but by the time he reached the dissecting rooms the little man had already opened the dreadful door and was heaving his bag inside.

'*Who are you?*' Utterson demanded.

But the little man, like Baxter before him, threw the door shut with a resounding clang.

Though not before Utterson had glimpsed, under the flare of a nearby street lamp, the most sooty, snarling, thoroughly *evil* visage he had seen since the days of Mr. Edward Hyde!

A Scouring Storm

THE POSSIBILITY THAT a man disguised as Jekyll had been joined by a man disguised as Mr. Hyde seemed to Utterson utterly absurd. But the idea that the impostor was transforming himself into a distorted mirror image, as Jekyll had done, seemed equally preposterous. So in the end Utterson had to reassure himself that the man he had seen disappearing into the dissecting rooms, while indisputably malevolent, was neither Jekyll nor Hyde. It was simply not the same man—or *men*.

Nevertheless, the speculations were all so unsettling that Utterson made no immediate attempt to return to the Jekyll home. Nor, however, did he spend much time at the premises of Utterson & Slaughter. His explanation to the firm's junior partner, Gideon Slaughter, was emphatic:

'Urgent business. A private matter.'

He visited Sir Palfrey Bramble in Park Lane, where the celebrated adventurer resided in a palatial mansion crowded with porcelain icons, Hindoo sculptures and mummified hunting trophies.

'Utterson, dear fellow! Come join me! I'll have some victuals brought in.' Bramble clapped hands to summon his silk-costumed servants.

Utterson shook his head. 'In normal circumstances I should enjoy nothing more, Sir Palfrey. But I have only a few questions to ask, and then I must be on my way.'

'Well take a seat, at least, old chap! Sit yourself down next to Pierre.'

Pierre was a stuffed Congolese gorilla with a missing left eye. The explorer himself, also missing a left eye, lowered his considerable bulk into a rattan armchair under a rhinoceros head.

'There was something you said in the street yesterday, Sir Palfrey.'

'Something I said indiscreet?' Years of rifle-blasts had deadened the old man's hearing.

'In the street,' Utterson repeated, more loudly. 'I believe you said something about Henry Jekyll.'

'Jekyll, you say? Well yes, quite remarkable, is it not? Quite remarkable!'

'May I ask what you have heard exactly?'

'Well, just that he's back in London of course—alive and well; back from the jaws of . . . whatever jaws he escaped from.'

'But who informed you of this news?'

'Who?' Sir Palfrey frowned. 'Well, I can't rightly remember, you know—these things get about by themselves, do they not? How did you find out?'

'I went to the Jekyll home,' Utterson said, 'only to have the door slammed in my face.'

'You don't say! Well, that's a bit rude of the old boy. Not some ill-feeling between the two of you, is there?'

'I shouldn't think so,' Utterson said. 'Jekyll himself—or at least the man calling himself Jekyll—assured me in a letter that we are still the best of friends.'

'But he's not yet paid you a visit?'

'None.'

'That's a bit rum, isn't it? When he's visited just about every-one else!'

A chill raced through Utterson. 'Are you saying, Sir Palfrey, that the man going by the name of Jekyll has done the rounds of the doctor's friends?'

'Dundered round the doctor's ends? What?'

'Has he visited his friends?' Utterson said, leaning forward. 'The men in Jekyll's circle?'

'Why yes—he was here not fifteen minutes ago! In this very room!'

Utterson felt dry-mouthed. 'He was here, you say?'

'Sitting where you are now.'

Utterson shifted uncomfortably; he had thought, upon sitting down, that the seat seemed warm. 'And what had he come to talk about?'

'What's that?' Sir Palfrey cupped a hand to his ear.

'I asked what the man calling himself Jekyll was talking about when he was here.'

'Oh, I don't know. Just reacquainting himself, I suppose. Hadn't been here for so long that he barely remembered the place. Very interested in my collections, he was.'

'Did he by any chance prevail upon you to sign an affidavit? Or any other papers?'

'Nothing of the sort. He was very good about the whole

thing. Just invited me to his dinner on Saturday. Only I shan't be going—my constitution and whatnot, you know. But Jekyll seemed not to mind.'

'Jekyll . . .' Utterson said, then shook himself. 'I assume you got a good look at the man?'

'Oh yes, yes.'

'And to your eyes did he resemble the real doctor?' asked Utterson—well aware that Sir Palfrey's vision was little more reliable than his hearing.

'Oh, well, you know . . . a fellow who's endured all that he has—you wouldn't expect him to look *exactly* the same, would you?'

Utterson leaned further forward. 'So he's *not* the same person, is he? He *doesn't* look like Henry, does he?'

'Oh, it's Henry all right,' Sir Palfrey said. 'I have a sense for such things. And so does Pierre. Between the two of us, with our two good eyes, we'd know if a man was a charlatan, wouldn't we?' And he winked—or blinked—at the stuffed gorilla.

'Well, of course you would.' Utterson rose, clapping on his hat. 'Then I'll waste no more of your time.'

'I say,' said the explorer, 'you're not put out by all this, are you? It must be difficult, I imagine, with all you had planned.'

'Planned?' Utterson repeated. 'And what, pray tell, am I suppose to have *planned*?'

But Palfrey, visibly self-conscious, got to his feet and muttered something expediently incomprehensible.

Utterson then headed for the book-crowded home of Professor Edmond Keyes in Cavendish Square. Of all the surviving members of Jekyll's circle it was Keyes, an historian of ancient mythology, who seemed to Utterson the least likely to be hood-winked by a fraudster.

'Yes, I heard the news.' Keyes was studying the proofs of his new monograph on Achelous. 'Though I can't say I gave it much credit at the time.'

'Of course you didn't,' said Utterson. 'You know as well as I that it cannot be true.'

'Now see here, Utterson, I said I didn't credit it *at the time*. But I've since met him in person. He called here, to this very room, and we spoke together at some length.'

'The fiend was here too?' Utterson asked, appalled.

'Fiend, Utterson? I'm not prepared to call him that.'

'But he was right here in this house?'

'Only an hour ago. Very persuasive he was, too. He knew things that only Jekyll could possibly know.'

'Such as what, may I ask?'

'Incidental details. Private details. About our mutual past. I shan't say more.'

Utterson elected not to pursue it. 'But he doesn't really *look* like Henry, does he?'

'Oh? Who told you that?'

'It's . . . just what I'm led to believe.'

'Well, I beg to differ. In fact, I'd have to say the resemblance was compelling.'

'Compelling?'

'Decidedly. And I'd be surprised if anyone thought differently. I'd be surprised if *you* did.'

Utterson was exasperated. 'But he's *not* Jekyll, don't you see? Whatever he looks like; however persuasive he might be.'

'Hmph,' Keyes said. 'The weight of numbers should tell a story. I'll be at his dinner on Saturday evening, as should you, Utterson, and if others of Jekyll's acquaintance are convinced he is who he claims to be, then I for one shan't be mounting a challenge. Nor should you, come to that. *Vir prudens non contra ventum mingit.*'

Utterson grunted. 'And what if I unmask him at the dinner, by the same token? I take it you will stand beside me then. You will not leave me to fight the beast alone?'

'If there's a Gorgon to be slain,' Keyes said, straightening his manuscript, 'then you can rely on me, dear fellow, to be the first to unsheathe my sword.'

But to Utterson he did not look like a man who was preparing for any sort of battle.

Utterson then visited Dr. Chauncey Wiseman in Henrietta Place; Dr. Hubert Frost in Savile Row; and Gareth Sessions, the eminent member of parliament, in Haverstock Hill; and in each case he found that the Jekyll claimant had already swept through like a scouring storm. Each of these men had conversed with him for some time; each seemed more or less satisfied as to the man's credibility; and each indicated that he was prepared, when the time came, to endorse him in whatever way necessary.

'But he's *not who he claims to be*,' Utterson insisted again and again. 'If he's anyone he's Dr. Guise—that's all he is. So why does everyone want to believe that he's Dr. Jekyll?'

'And why,' returned Sessions pointedly, 'do you so passionately want to believe that he's not?'

Utterson made one final visit to his home in Gaunt Street, lest the impostor had dropped in on his rounds of Jekyll's friends. But Poole seemed surprised.

'Visitors? Why no, sir. Is there anyone I should be expecting?'

'Just be on your guard,' Utterson told him. 'And be especially careful about believing in fairy tales.'

At the telegraph office, just before closing time, he dispatched a cable to Richard Enfield:

STRANGE COMPLICATIONS STOP IMPOSTOR OCCUPYING JEKYLL HOME STOP DESCRIPTION NECESSARY OF INQUISITIVE MAN MET AT YOUR CLUB STOP GRATEFUL IN ADVANCE UTTERSON

It was a wild bid. He knew that before embarking for France Enfield was passing several days in Dover—possibly renewing acquaintances with an erstwhile lover—but he was not certain of his lodging place (on a hunch he addressed the telegram to the Lord Warden Hotel, which his kinsman had mentioned favourably). Nevertheless he was oddly convinced that the prying stranger whom Enfield had encountered at his club was somehow related to the claimant, if indeed he were not the claimant himself; and now his only regret was that he had not enquired further while he had the opportunity.

Whatever the case, it would be good to renew contact with someone—*anyone*—who might take his side. Increasingly friendless in London, Utterson hungered desperately for support as he prepared for the claimant's dinner. Hercules himself, as Professor Keyes would have attested, must surely have shivered before facing his labours alone.

A Tempest of Emotions

THERE WAS A time when dinners at Jekyll's house were the chief jewels of the social season. Utterson looked forward to them as he might a royal banquet, savoured them in the moment like a vintage wine, then kindled the memories for weeks—*months*—afterwards.

On this Saturday, however, he arrived at his home at Gaunt Street at six o'clock, opened the door guardedly, ascended on hushed feet to his bedroom, brushed his tailcoat, affixed his tie and cufflinks, and uncapped a decanter of bedside gin to settle his nerves. His hands, he noticed, were shaking uncontrollably.

'Will sir be requiring dinner this evening?' Poole asked from the door.

Utterson hurriedly concealed the glass. 'Not tonight, Poole,' he managed. 'I'm dining with old friends.'

'Old friends, sir?'

'All rather unexpected, which is why I failed to inform you.'

'Very well, sir—I take it you'll be returning late?'

'Very late, I expect. If you've prepared something for dinner you may enjoy it yourself.'

'Why thank you, sir.'

In the cab, still trembling, Utterson could not prevent his mind from reliving a high tea of exceptional awkwardness that he had shared that very afternoon with the widow Spratling.

It was at the tea rooms of the Savoy Hotel, the sort of fashionable establishment he would never have patronised had he not been seeking to impress a lady. The widow, still in mourning silks, and looking indecently alluring even under the hideous glare of the hotel's electric lamps, was accompanied as usual by her smirking son Terrence and was wearing on her countenance an expression of great expectation.

'You said last week you had some pleasing news for me, Gabriel.'

'That I did . . .'

'And yet you have already been so good to me that I don't know how I might ever repay you.'

'You should not even think about repaying me, Nora.'

'But I do think about it, Gabriel. Every day I say to Terrence that we have been delivered an angel. I say to him that we should never despair if things look bleak, because Gabriel will find a way to extricate us from our misery.'

'You should not elevate me to such levels,' Utterson said stiffly. 'Indeed, I fear I might yet prove something of a disappointment to you, for a certain announcement I had intended to make might need to be postponed.'

'Oh?' The widow's face wrinkled.

'Well,' conceded Utterson, 'it's just a temporary setback, I hope, and I am doing everything to settle the matter expeditiously. Nonetheless, it means I am unable to play the angelic role you have generously ascribed to me. So I trust you will forgive me.'

'Of course I forgive you, Gabriel—how could I not?' Nora paused, clearly struggling to contain her curiosity. 'But whatever could it be,' she went on finally, 'that you were intending to announce to me? I hope it is not improper to ask?'

Stung by her plaintive tone, and melted by the anguish in her eyes, Utterson found himself divulging his little secret. 'Well,' he said, 'I suppose there's no harm in telling you. You see, I had been intending to move personally into the Jekyll home next week, once it legally became my property, leaving my current abode in Gaunt Street vacant for the two of you.'

The widow gasped. 'You mean to say you would offer your own home to Terrence and me?'

'Precisely.'

She beamed. 'Good Lord, Gabriel—could it possibly be true?'

'It has been my intention for some time now.'

'But how would I ever afford the rent for such a fine house, in the straits I am in?'

'I expect no rent at all,' said Utterson. 'In fact, it is you who would be doing a favour for me, as I do not wish to part with the place entirely; nor can I conceive of tenants more reliable than you and Terrence.'

'Oh, it's true, Gabriel—it's true! We would care for the place as our own! Why, this is exactly the news we have been waiting to hear. A home in Gaunt Street! This is just what I have been dreaming of—to get away from that stinking, noisy hovel in

Shepherd's Bush. Oh Gabriel, make no mistake, you are an angel indeed!'

Utterson was already regretting his disclosure. 'And yet,' he warned, 'there might well be a delay, as I've indicated—perhaps a serious one.'

'But how could it be, Gabriel? What could possibly thwart us?'

Utterson sighed. 'It's all very silly,' he said. 'You see, a man—an impostor—has moved into the Jekyll home, claiming it as his own.'

'An impostor?'

'A man claiming to be Henry Jekyll.'

'Henry Jekyll! *Our* Henry?'

'A fraudster,' Utterson insisted. 'A brazen, black-hearted fraudster.'

The widow frowned, thinking about it. 'But if he's a fraudster, dear Gabriel, then why have you not had him evicted?'

'Whoever he is, he has managed to hoodwink many of those who have met him—mainly old men with failing memories.'

'But not you?'

'Not I,' sniffed Utterson. 'I shall confront him shortly.'

'So you've not yet seen him?'

'I shall do so tonight, at dinner.'

'At dinner, you say? You're going to meet this fraudster over dinner?'

Utterson realised how far-fetched it all sounded. 'I shall deal with him there.'

The widow looked uncertain. 'And you are absolutely *sure* he's not Henry?'

'Entirely.'

'Even though Henry's body was never discovered?'

'His body . . . his body does not *need* to be discovered.'

'And though you admit you have no real proof that Henry is dead?'

'I had no *need* of proof. None, I tell you. Because I *know* Henry Jekyll is dead. And I *know* that his friends have been deceived. I know this for a fact.'

There followed an excruciating silence, during which the widow appeared increasingly distant. 'Henry Jekyll . . .' she whispered.

'Not Jekyll,' Utterson said. 'A charlatan.'

But the widow seemed not to have heard him. She seemed, indeed, to have fallen into a trance.

And Utterson, in that dreadful moment, understood that Nora, too, wanted to believe, for her own reasons, that Henry Jekyll was still alive.

Because, by God, she's still in love with him.

All these thoughts were scraping through his head as the cab wheeled into Jekyll's street, where a sudden chill would years earlier have made the amber glow of the doctor's windows seem inordinately inviting. Tonight, however, through a tempest of emotions, they resembled to Utterson nothing less than the fires of hell.

Through Blurred Vision

UTTERSON'S FIRST SURPRISE was that the impertinent Baxter was nowhere to be seen. Greeting him at the door was an immaculately groomed manservant of perfect bearing and manners, while down the passage a couple of freshly scrubbed kitchenmaids were bustling into the kitchen—hired staff, he assumed, engaged exclusively for the occasion.

His second surprise was that all the articles of furniture that had been hibernating in the dissecting rooms—mahogany chairs, an ornate umbrella stand, paintings of foxhunts—had been returned to their place in the entrance hall, and with remarkable accuracy at that; as if, indeed, they had never been anywhere else.

Unnerved and indignant—for the restoration of Jekyll's place was a pleasure he had been reserving for himself—Utterson became aware of voices in the front parlour: men chatting and joking as though they were at a race meeting. A pall of cigar smoke as thick as church incense. The sizzle of fat from the kitchens. And then, just as he was polishing his spectacles—the rapid contrast between exterior and interior temperatures had misted the lenses—he heard a strikingly familiar voice:

'Utterson, old chap! My word, it's good to see your face again!'

Utterson wheeled around and saw, through blurred vision, a figure swooping across the hall to greet him.

'Has it really been seven years?'

Then, before he could summon the snide response he had been brewing for days—'Have we met, sir?'—he prodded the spectacles up his nose and beheld a figure who seemed to have been recreated from his most cherished memories.

The same broad shoulders and sporting physique, the same flashing brown irises and flared black eyebrows, the same knavish smile, the same wine-stained lips and dusky skin, the same thick crop of oiled-back hair silvering at the sides. And all of it resplendent in tail coat, wing-collar shirt and black necktie—items lifted directly, it seemed, from the doctor's wardrobe.

Henry Jekyll, like his entrance hall, had been restored with unerring accuracy.

'What's the matter, old fellow? You've not pawned that silver tongue of yours, I hope?'

'N-n-no,' Utterson managed, shaking the man's hand. 'I'm not late, am I?'

'Late?' The claimant laughed. 'No timepiece in London is more reliable than Gabriel Utterson! Come this way, good fellow, we've just been talking about you.'

And with that the lawyer found himself being guided down the passage as the claimant mumbled apologies in his ear:

'Sorry about Baxter again, old chap, but you must understand the man was never intended to be a butler. He was a merchant seaman when I first took him in, so his manners are not quite what they should be. And my most heartfelt apologies, too, for not paying you a visit in recent days. But I'm led to understand you've engaged Poole as your butler, and I didn't want to risk running into the old fellow alone. Poole always thought so absurdly highly of me that I'm not at all sure how he will receive the news of my return. He can be surprisingly emotional in his way.'

'He saw your envelope,' Utterson murmured.

'What's that?'

'I said he saw your envelope—the handwriting.'

'So he knows already that I'm back, does he?'

'He said . . . something.'

'Well, I should have guessed. He never did miss much, did old Poole.'

But then, as if hearing the conversation from afar, Utterson with a shock became aware that he was already being lured into the impostor's trap. For he had been so disarmed by the physical similarity, not to mention the warm tone of familiarity, that he was responding to the claimant as if he really *were* Henry Jekyll.

But now he was entering the parlour, where he saw Hubert Frost and Chauncey Wiseman chatting convivially; Edmond Keyes was smoking in the corner with Roderick Godfreys, QC; while Hubert Tilley, the royal portrait artist, and Christopher Piggott, the writer of renown, were inspecting a china vase. And all these men paused for a moment to register Utterson's arrival and murmur guarded greetings and shift awkwardly around the room, while the claimant, doing the rounds, continued laughing and reminiscing and occasionally glancing in Utterson's direction as if for approval. The lawyer himself, meanwhile, having recovered from his initial shock, stared back at the man with mounting annoyance, for he could see now that the fellow resembled Henry Jekyll just *too* accurately to be credible. It was as if he had *groomed* himself to look precisely like the only surviving image of Jekyll (a photographic portrait from the Royal College of Surgeons). But under the glare of the gas bracket it was clear that his complexion owed much to the application of theatrical powders, that his hair had been darkened as if with India ink, and that his every gesture was unnaturally studied, as if he were performing Jekyll's mannerisms like stage directions in a play.

It was *not* Jekyll, and Utterson *knew* it. So why were the others so damnably receptive?

A bell tinkled and the men repaired as one to the dining room, where Jekyll's magnificent rosewood table had been dressed in satin napery and set with the house's finest crockery and services. There was even an uncorked bottle of Bouchard that Utterson had been planning to savour ever since he discovered it, years earlier, in the cellar.

The claimant took to the head of the table with Utterson facing him from the polar end; the others settled in at the sides; the apricot-shaded lamps cast a salmony glow across the room; and from the kitchens in succession came oxtail soup, Welsh rarebit, fried oysters, mutton chops, widgeon, braised pheasant, stewed pickles and devilled ice cream.

But Utterson ate sparingly and drank not at all, waiting impatiently for an *après-dîner* moment when he could confront the impostor alone. And in the meantime he had to content himself with observing the man's fabricated enthusiasm, his counterfeit manners and his outrageously contrived 'explanation'.

'Now I've no doubt you've many questions to ask about my disappearance,' the man said, stubbing his cigar, 'and to some extent I hope I've already answered them in person. Yet I'm afraid that there remain many points upon which my account is going to remain insubstantial, even entirely unsatisfactory, owing to the severity of the injuries to my memory.'

Utterson could not resist a snort at this and the others glanced at him sharply.

'Yes,' the claimant said, looking humbled, 'I know very well how inadequate it all sounds, but alas there is little more that I can do. I fear there are some broken bridges in my mind that will never be repaired, and some threads in the fabric of my memory that can never be re-sewn. But please do not be fooled by my appearance, gentlemen, for the truth is you are dining tonight with a very sick man.'

'Sick, are you?' Utterson said.

'Sick, indeed,' said the claimant, sighing, and for a moment seemed as though he could not summon the strength to continue. 'And it all began,' he went on finally, 'with that man of the most loathsome character, that scoundrel whose nature was immediately apparent to all who met him—and whose nature, more to the point, was immediately apparent to me . . .'

Thinking for a moment, illogical as it was, that the claimant was about to admit his peculiar relationship with Hyde—that Jekyll *was* Hyde—Utterson held his breath. But then the man continued:

'Well, perhaps it starts earlier than Hyde,' he admitted. 'With my experiments in the field of transformative potions. Some of you know better than others what I'm talking about, but in truth I was always very guarded about the scale of my ambitions, even with my closest friends. For I was determined, you see, to produce chemical formulae that would transform the nature of man, potions that would drain him of his most violent impulses, and turn the most inveterate villains into men of virtue. But alas, there was always a certain impediment to my success, for naturally I needed a subject—one man, at least, upon whom I could test the efficacy of my brews.'

The claimant paused, looking anguished again, and for a moment it seemed that he was about to admit his great secret: '*So I resolved to test the potion upon myself.*' And again Utterson had to remind himself that this was *not* the real Jekyll.

'But then, at some devilish hour of the morning,' the man went on, 'I was out walking the streets, trying to clear my head, when I chanced upon a most violent and horrible scene. In the mouth of an alley, at the back of some crumbling block of storehouses, a little man in a greatcoat was thrashing a young urchin with his stick, and repeatedly kicking him in the ribs. Now my first reaction was naturally to restrain the brute; and so, together with a passing stranger, I collared him and held him down, though he was struggling like a wildcat. We intended to hail a constable—the urchin, who turned out to be a pickpocket, had already bolted—but we could not find one in that barren district, as much as we hollered. So we resolved to detain the villain temporarily, until the police could be called, and seeing my house was closest we went there, making a gaol of sorts out of my dissecting rooms; and it was there, for better or worse, that I became better acquainted with the little fellow.'

The claimant, clearly aware that he had his guests spellbound, pursed his dark lips as if tasting his own disdain.

'The other man, being a baker, needed to head off and attend to his trade, meaning I was left alone with the brute;

and listening as he railed against the world in general, and sensing the palpable malevolence that he exuded like a musk, and understanding, by the course of his ramblings, that he was an ex-convict of no fixed address, destined it seemed to some further mayhem . . . well, I was struck by an entirely new possibility. For it seemed to me that now, literally within my grasp, was the answer to all my problems. Indeed, it was as if Providence had furnished me with this little monster, specifically that in him I might gain a subject for my chemical experiments.'

The only sound was the tick of Jekyll's clock in the hall.

The claimant sighed. 'So I made a pact with the fellow. I told him I would not turn him over to the police, as I had every right to do, if he would only agree to partake of my formulae. I offered him board and money for the duration, even a stake in my inheritance, in return for his obedience and silence. And though the villain was understandably leery at first, he accepted the terms of my offer, which of course could never be committed formally on paper.

'And so began my efforts to change the bestial nature of "Mr. Hyde"—this being the new name which I had given him—by summoning from their slumber the man's more virtuous qualities, and simultaneously exorcising his more destructive demons.

'I rented some dingy rooms in Soho, which served as his lodgings, and in secret, late at night, he would present himself at my house, entering through the door of the dissecting rooms, to ingest my potions. Now I cannot claim my success was immediate, for there was much trial and error, but it seemed to me that within a matter of months Mr. Hyde became a different man, a more agreeable man, capable of compassion and flashes of wit— so much so that I genuinely believed I was changing him for the better. And though this was all so profound that at times I was tempted to shout "Eureka!", I still could not be certain, because it was possible that the improvements in his demeanour were merely a response to the security and friendship that I had bestowed upon him. So I secretly began to administer to him placebo mixtures—foaming water with no real transformative properties—simply to see if the absence of the genuine potion would return the man to his former state . . .'

The claimant now shook his head grimly, as though he could barely continue.

'Now I do not need to tell you gentlemen that it was during these dark periods, when he was not taking my corrective medicines, that he gave himself over to the most violent of rages. It was certainly during this time that some of you encountered him, and clearly could not help wondering about the nature of my business with such a beast. Indeed, his evil seemed even more pronounced than it had been previously, as if the devil inside were trying to make up for lost time. And it was in one of these rages, I regret to say, that he struck down and murdered Sir Danvers Carew . . .'

The silence throughout the house was now uncanny—even the clock, it seemed, had ceased ticking.

'I was shattered. I had never expected it to come to this. Of course I vowed to have him arrested forthwith—how could it be any other way? And yet when Hyde appeared before me, after the crime, he blamed the potions I had prepared for him, saying they had given him the most violent headaches and nausea, which in turn had made him lose control of his senses. He was in a state of pure delirium, he said, when he attacked Sir

Danvers—he did not even know what he was doing. And I could see how this might be so—that the sudden change in dosage might have caused him to unravel—and I further saw that, if that were indeed the case, then I myself was partially responsible for his actions. And so, for better or worse, I elected to continue my treatment of Mr. Hyde, if only so I could reel him back from iniquity while there was still time, and then throw both of us before the mercy of the law.

'So I redoubled my efforts, with appreciable success; and just when I was thinking I had done all that I could possibly do, I became aware of some others, former associates of the fellow's, who seeing their old companion living in such luxury, had set their minds on taking advantage of him.'

The claimant looked around with pained eyes.

'Now this caused Hyde much anxiety, for he had no desire to be dragged back into their midst; and it gave me even greater distress, for I could not allow these blackguards to undo everything I had been striving to achieve. So when these rogues summoned Hyde to Soho, in order to perpetrate some sort of blackmail, I foolishly went in his place, armed but alone, intending to put an end to the matter once and for all. But I had not gone long into the confrontation—of which I remember very little—when they blackjacked me and dumped my body on a coal-steamer moored in the Thames. And so it was that I awoke in Lisbon, with no idea how I came to be there, unable to remember who I was or where I had come from—insensible to anything but the gnawing suspicion that it would be unsafe for me to return to London.

'Hyde meanwhile gave himself over to suicide—I did not learn this until very recently—and I was classified as missing.

And missing I was indeed for many years, gentlemen, even to myself. I had the good fortune, however, to fall in with a small community of English fugitives—even now I do not know their real names—who gave me shelter and sustenance for a while, and slowly my skills in surgery returned, so that I was able to apply myself gainfully to my trade, becoming a roving physician, engaging in many surgeries and adventures across the breadth of the Peninsula. And eventually the fragments of my memory reassembled sufficiently for me to recall who I was, and what had happened to me, and I resolved to return at once to London, and reclaim my former existence, apologise to all I needed to apologise to, face up to any punishment that was necessary, while working tirelessly to restore my good name.'

The claimant looked around the table imploringly, then raised a glass in his yellowed fingers.

'So here I am before you now, gentlemen, seeking redemption for my days of shame. And if some of my memories occasionally sputter, and if some of them remain shrouded for ever in oblivion, I trust you will forgive me. For I am fractured, yes, and incomplete, no doubt, but I remain in word and spirit your true friend Henry Jekyll—and I propose we make a toast of it.'

And such was his conviction during this remarkable performance that the other men at the table, most of whom were by varying degrees inebriated, raised their glasses approvingly—Roderick Godfreys even muttered 'Hear, hear'—and toasted the good doctor and his unimpeachable ambitions. But after the glasses clinked and were lowered again, no one was surprised to see that Mr. Utterson had remained rigid in his seat, his glass untouched, his mouth compressed and his eyes burning like coals.

The Warmth of Fire and Wine

THE OTHERS RETIRED by degrees, though Hubert Tilley lingered disagreeably for a while; but finally, with
the house staff also gone, there remained just two men
in the old house, not accounting for whoever might have been
lurking in the shadows of neighbouring rooms.

The lawyer and the claimant took their places besides Jekyll's
hearth, where a well-stoked fire was blazing, and the master of
the house poured some wine, which Utterson swilled in his glass
before taking a few experimental sips; and—just as he had on
innumerable occasions in the past, after an excellent dinner—he
listened attentively as the doctor made a confession.

'This is very awkward, Utterson. It seems that I have the
support of everyone in my circle, and yet you, my closest friend,
remain the inflexible sceptic.'

Utterson smirked. 'I have found from past experience that it
pays to be the inflexible sceptic.'

'Of course it does; and in many ways I would have expected
nothing less. Still, under the circumstances I cannot just tip my
hat to you at the crossroads, as it were, but rather make it my
intention to win you over; for only then will I feel that I have
truly returned.'

'You will not win me over, whoever you are,' replied Utterson. 'Your scheme will break apart and this house will never be yours—you may depend on it.'

The claimant nodded gravely. 'Then it is even worse than I thought,' he said. 'And yet I can see how my reappearance might be unwelcome to you, for various personal reasons. Nonetheless, you must know that I am prepared to reward you richly for your assistance, should you agree to help me—for you remain, apart from anything else, my trusted legal adviser.'

'Reward me richly?' Utterson could scarcely believe it. 'You think this is all about finances, do you? And you really think I would be prepared to counsel you, and act on your behalf? By Jove, you are more brazen than I thought.'

'Utterson, you must believe me, it is not a matter of buying you off. Perhaps I've expressed myself poorly. It's just that you must have had certain plans, I understand that, and I am fully prepared to compensate you for your inconvenience. As a businessman and a friend.'

Utterson chuckled mirthlessly. 'Then I must congratulate you, sir.'

'Congratulate me . . .?'

'Congratulate you, yes, on how far you've managed to proceed with this flagrant little charade. No one could ever accuse you of lacking audacity—or of being ill-prepared, for that matter. Indeed, if I did not know better even *I* might have been taken in. But you must know that could never happen. Because I alone am in possession of a certain document, you see—a document written by the one and only Henry Jekyll. The *real* Henry Jekyll.'

The claimant nodded. 'In point of fact, I wrote that will when I was heading out to confront Hyde's blackmailers. I did not want the burden of my estate resting on Hyde's shoulders, making him vulnerable to the schemes of his friends, so I altered the terms of my will so that you became my sole beneficiary. But had I returned from that fateful meeting I would certainly have destroyed the document—it was never meant to be implemented, I regret to say.'

'Oh, I'm not talking about the will,' Utterson said, and the fire crackled wickedly. 'And this is where all your preparation will do you no good, whoever you are. For there is *another* document I collected from the dissecting rooms on that terrible night—*another* document written by Henry Jekyll.'

'Another document?' asked the claimant.

'Indeed,' said Utterson. 'A statement—a confession, if you like—written in the hand of Henry Jekyll.'

'A statement?'

'That is what I said.'

'And you are in possession of this statement?'

'Safely secured.'

'And what is the substance of this statement?'

'Surely you can tell me.'

'I beg your pardon?'

'Well, Henry Jekyll wrote it, so Henry Jekyll must know its contents.'

The claimant shook his head. 'I'm afraid I remember nothing of a second statement.'

Utterson smirked. 'Of course you don't—because *you* never wrote it.'

For a while the only sounds came from the fire and the whistling wind. Then the claimant shook his head. 'This is a most serious business, Utterson.'

'I cannot disagree with that.'

'You seem to be suggesting that this document is significant.'

'It is very significant.'

'Significant enough to be used against me in court?'

'It would demolish you,' said Utterson.

'I see.' The claimant looked into his wine. 'Then I really wish I could remember writing such a document.'

'Try as hard as you like, you will never succeed.'

'Of course, I cannot fully account for my state of mind at the time. But I do seem to recall, during my meeting with the blackmailers, having some blank paper thrust in front of me.'

'Oh,' said Utterson, chuckling, 'so you intend to claim that you wrote the statement under duress, is that it?'

'If I wrote it at all, that seems the most likely explanation.'

'You wrote it, all right,' insisted Utterson, before correcting himself: 'I mean . . . Jekyll wrote it.'

The claimant shrugged. 'Well, it could have been Hyde's work, of course. He was, in point of fact, very practised in the forger's art.'

'Oh really?' said Utterson. 'And what possible reason would Hyde have for forging such a statement?'

'Well, I don't know what the statement says—since you refuse to tell me—but I can conceive of any number of reasons. He may, for instance, have been trying to protect himself.'

'There is nothing in the statement that could protect Hyde,' Utterson assured him.

'Or perhaps he was *forced* into writing the statement—forced by his blackmailers, I mean, in order to account for his suicide. And for my own disappearance at the same time.'

'Well that, too, is . . .'

But Utterson trailed off, realising that such an explanation might indeed be dressed up to sound credible in court. *A ludicrous farrago of lies, my lord, designed to throw the law off the scent.* He needed to be more prudent; he had conceivably revealed too much already.

'It matters not,' he said instead. 'The statement itself attests to your lies. But there are numerous other ways your story can be dismantled.'

'If you refer to my memory, dear Utterson, I have already spoken of the fragmentary nature of that.'

'Yes, and very convenient that is, too. Do you recall, by any chance, our days at Cambridge?'

'Of course I do.'

'And do you happen to remember the night we took a short-cut through the graveyard of St Giles?'

'I have a vague memory of such a thing . . .'

'Then you will remember what happened there, amid the graves.'

The claimant looked uncomfortable. 'Is this really important?'

'You remember nothing at all?'

'I'm afraid not.'

'What about the sexton who rescued us? Do you not remember his name?'

'Nor that, as it happens. But all this was many years ago, Utterson, and not worth remembering, even if my memory had not been impaired.'

'Not worth remembering, you say? Henry Jekyll would *never* forget the events of that night.'

'Perhaps Henry Jekyll doesn't want to.'

Utterson huffed. 'Well, what about our visit to Brighton, then—our famous sojourn to Brighton? Do you remember that?'

'Again, most vaguely.'

'And do you recall the name of the young lady you courted there?'

'It was Lucy Thicke, was it not?'

'It was Lizzie Thorn—how could you not remember that?'

'Lizzie Thorn?' The claimant frowned.

'None other. The *real* Henry Jekyll would never have forgotten that.'

'But I'm afraid you're mistaken, dear Utterson.'

'*I'm* mistaken?'

'Why yes,' the claimant said. 'Lizzie Thorn was the name of a young maiden at Bristol—do you not remember? But it was Lucy Thicke, certainly Lucy Thicke, whom I romanced in Brighton.'

'Oh yes?' said Utterson. 'Oh yes?'

But then—in a moment of unspeakable horror—Utterson realised that the claimant was right.

'I take no pleasure in correcting you, dear Utterson,' the man said, with a twinkle in his eyes. 'But it only proves, does it not, that all men's memories can become unreliable in the haze of the past?'

Utterson suddenly felt starved of air. The fire was leaping and laughing. The clock was ticking thunderously. And the claimant himself . . . the claimant had such a malicious, mocking curl to his lips that suddenly Utterson could not tolerate it. A strange impulse seized him.

He lunged forward and stabbed a finger at the claimant's cheek, then dragged it across the dusky skin and held it up triumphantly, expecting to see a smear of powder on the tip.

But there was no powder. There was nothing at all.

The claimant, investigating his face as though for a wound, looked perplexed. 'My dear Utterson,' he said, 'is there some kind of point to this?'

But Utterson, inhaling a lungful of the heated air, could not answer. He straightened but felt remarkably dizzy; he swayed on his feet and the room tilted around him; he glared at the claimant through swimming eyes.

'You will never get away with it,' he declared. 'You will never get away with it, I tell you!'

Then, lest he topple over, he wrenched himself from the room, bustled down the stairs, collected his hat and monkey-headed cane, and burst from the vestibule into the cold of the street, where his breath rose like the clouds of a steam engine.

Day of Agitation

UTTERSON'S SLEEP THAT night was so profound that he became convinced that something had been stirred into his drink. For how else could he explain it? With his mind as agitated as it had ever been, it was inconceivable that he would plunge so quickly into oblivion. Moreover there had been a metallic undertaste to the wine that in retrospect seemed highly suspect. And Jekyll had always been adept at mixing potions (*no—not Jekyll*, he forcibly had to remind himself, *but the impostor who's taken his place*).

In any case, he remembered nothing in the morning save a vivid dream in which Jekyll had not killed himself in the person of Mr. Hyde, but had survived, confessed his crimes to the world, and engaged Utterson to defend him in the Old Bailey.

'Gentlemen of the jury'—Utterson was in wig and gown for the first time in decades—'you see before you a man of peerless integrity, of the highest order, a Fellow of the Royal Society no less, who has been charged with some of the most heinous crimes ever to have been brought before this court. But I ask you, is it really Dr. Jekyll who should be here in the dock today? Or is it the second being, the one who is called Mr. Hyde? For it was Hyde, was it not, who enacted the crimes for which Jekyll is now being tried? It was Hyde who murdered, bludgeoned and thieved. And yet where is this Mr. Hyde I speak of? Is he visible before you? No, indeed, he is not. For Hyde is concealed deep within Dr. Jekyll, and safely imprisoned there at that. He is a scoundrel and a malefactor, true, but no more evil or dangerous than all the other scoundrels and malefactors that today lie hidden in this very court. For whom among you does not harbour his own Mr. Hyde? And who does not sometimes hear his Hyde pounding against the walls of his cell? Who does not daily, hourly, suppress the urges of his horrible Hyde?

'No,' said Utterson, 'Henry Jekyll's only crime, it seems to me, was to experiment upon himself in order to test the security of the prison; and that Mr. Hyde escaped so violently only justifies the urgency of the inspection. So while you have every reason to deliver a verdict on Mr. Hyde, you can no more condemn Dr. Jekyll than you can condemn yourselves. We are all Jekylls, yea, but equally we are all Hydes.'

Presently the bells sounded nine o'clock. Utterson jolted—he had not overslept in years—and dressed in uncommon haste, buttoning his clothes even as he was stumbling down the stairs.

'Is sir unwell?' asked Poole in the hall.

'Why do you ask, Poole?'

'I heard you crash around last night, and collapse onto your bed.'

'I was out of sorts, it's true.'

'And afterwards I heard you moving about.'

'It's possible,' Utterson admitted, though he remembered no such thing. 'But I've no time to talk now, Poole—I'm late for church.'

When he arrived at St Mary's the deacon was already reading from Genesis.

'And Jacob said to Rebekah his mother, Behold, Esau my brother is a hairy man, and I am a smooth man; my father peradventure will feel me, and I shall seem to him a deceiver; and I shall bring a curse upon me, and not a blessing.'

But Utterson was not listening. Of all the events of the previous evening, and all the lies that had been loosed, there was one exchange that had taken hold of his imagination. It was the claimant's preposterous explanation for his failure to visit Gaunt Street: *'I didn't want to risk running into the old fellow alone. Poole always thought so absurdly highly of me that I'm not sure at all how he will receive the news of my return.'*

At the time Utterson had paid it scant attention, still warding off the claimant's redoubtable charm. But now, installed in his customary pew in St Mary's, he found an entirely more plausible explanation: the impostor did not want to face Poole because his butler, of all men, would never be deceived by him. *That* was the real reason for the impostor's reluctance—not some sensitivity to the old man's emotions.

'A curse on him!' Utterson hissed, before coming to his senses and nodding apologetically to his fellow worshippers.

Nevertheless he sprang to his feet as soon as the blessing was over and marched resolutely back to Gaunt Street, where he found Poole scrubbing wine stains from the stairs—not that he could remember spilling anything.

'Never mind that, Poole, I want you to come with me.'

'Sir?'

'Put down that bucket, I say—we're going for a ride.'

'A ride, sir? In a carriage, sir?'

'I know this is a surprise'—in fact, the two men had not trav-elled together in years—'but there's no need to change your clothes. I merely want you to see something.'

Fifteen minutes later they were bowling along through the frost-pinched streets. 'Is it something to do with your illness, sir?' Poole ventured.

'Illness?'

'You said you were feeling out of sorts, sir. I wondered if it had something to do with your dinner last night.'

'I suppose you could say that.'

'Something you ate, sir?'

'No . . . something . . .' Utterson glanced at his butler and resolved to tell the truth. 'We're going to Jekyll's, Poole, that's where we're going—to the home of Henry Jekyll.'

'Sir?'

'In response to a rather disagreeable complication.'

'What has happened, sir?' the butler asked, genuinely concerned.

'Well, first of all I must own that I've not been completely honest with you, Poole. Do you remember that letter I received on Wednesday—the one you thought was in Jekyll's handwriting?'

'I remember.'

'What if I were to tell you that it was a clever forgery—the work of a man claiming to be the missing doctor?'

'A man claiming to be Dr. Jekyll!'

'Indeed. And what if I were to tell you that this shame-less impostor has moved into the Jekyll home, which he claims is his own?'

'You mean to say there is a man is pretending to be my master? And he has taken over his house?'

'Precisely so.'

'The devil!' Poole said, sitting forward in his seat with fists clenched. And Utterson remembered, with considerable satisfaction, that this was the same man who seven years earlier, fearing Mr. Hyde had harmed his master, had taken an axe to the laboratory door with frightening fury.

'The devil is right, Poole,' said Utterson. 'As you will shortly see for yourself.'

Above Jekyll's street a flock of ravens was circling like buzzards. Milky sunlight was straining through gauze-like clouds. Utterson, inflating his chest like a pigeon, ascended the stairs and rapped on the door with his ostrich-headed cane. Then he turned to Poole.

'The impostor has a butler,' he warned. 'A scoundrel called Baxter.'

'A butler!'

'Who does not even pretend to look like you, Poole. Still, you should prepare yourself lest—'

But then the bolts clicked and the great door squeaked open. Utterson wheeled around, expecting to find Baxter on the threshold. But instead, to his unwelcome surprise, he saw it was the claimant himself, resplendent in a mulberry coat and beaver-skin hat.

'Utterson!' the man exclaimed. 'What are you doing here?'

'Oh, it's you, is it?'

'I'm about to head out, dear fellow—why?'

'Why?' Utterson snorted. 'Because I've brought someone with me, that's why—a man you seem determined to avoid!'

And with that he peeled aside, holding one arm extended lest Poole make an indignant charge, and watched as the claimant's face squinted momentarily before igniting with delight.

'*Poole!*' the man cried. 'My good man Poole!'

Utterson turned, expecting to find the old butler suitably enraged. But to his chagrin Poole merely looked disconcerted.

'Master . . .?' The butler was agape.

'Poole!' the claimant said again. 'My word, it's good to see that ugly mug of yours.'

'Master . . . is it truly you?'

'Your old guv'nor, Poole, back in his London castle!'

The claimant stepped forward and seized Poole's hands and shook them vigorously; and Poole, to Utterson's mounting dismay, simply stood there, dumbstruck, with a tear glistening in his eye—as if it really were Henry Jekyll who was greeting him on the steps.

'I'm sorry I've not yet come to visit, old bean.'

'Think nothing of it, master!'

The salutations, the grinning, the shaking of hands and the chuckling continued for what seemed an eternity; and it was only fifteen minutes later, when they were returning home in the cab, that Poole belatedly acknowledged some regret.

'I don't know, sir,' he admitted sheepishly. 'He *did* look like Dr. Jekyll . . . and all his expressions and such, they were exactly the same. Exactly the same, sir.' He sighed. 'Well, we were very close, my master and me, and well, we were twenty whole years together . . . and, well, you know how it is, sir.'

Utterson just stared out of the window, his eyes narrowed to slits.

Till the Heavens Fall

A CODICIL TO JEKYLL'S will entitled Utterson to the full estate—property as well as half a million in sterling—three months after the doctor's disappearance. But the lawyer had elected not to pursue this avenue (he destroyed the codicil entirely) so as not, ironically, to arouse any undue suspicion. And now, after waiting almost seven years to see Henry Jekyll declared dead *in absentia*, his rightful bequest was in danger of being ripped away, just five days before it was officially his, by a fiendish fraudster and a circle of friends who seemed inordinately disposed in the man's favour. Not only that, but the unexpected response of Poole, on top of all else, now seemed the ultimate betrayal—for if a man cannot trust his butler, Utterson thought, then on whom can he rely?

What he needed, he decided, was someone who had known the doctor even more intimately than Poole. Hastie Lanyon had been Jekyll's personal physician for a while, but he of course had been dead for some years. As for his replacement, Utterson had an idea that Jekyll had engaged a foreign doctor—some barely qualified fellow—but what in blazes was his name? He visited his files, where he kept a long list of Jekyll's creditors, and eventually unearthed the answer—a bill in the name of one H. Preiss, MD, of Shoreditch.

He was at the address—an ugly modern abode with oversized windows—within ninety minutes. A severe looking *hausfrau* answered the door.

'I am looking for a certain Dr. Preiss,' he told her. 'Might you know of his whereabouts?'

'Who is asking, please?'

'Mr. Gabriel Utterson, lawyer of the City.'

The *hausfrau* withdrew into the darkness; there was some guttural whispering and shuffling; and a bearded, bespectacled gentleman smoking a meerschaum pipe waddled to the door.

'You seek Herman Preiss?' he asked, in an accent as thick as pumpernickel. 'That is correct.'

'Then I cannot help you, sir—the doctor no longer lives here.'

'Do you know where he resides now?'

'The doctor is missing.'

'Missing? For how long?'

'For six months.'

'And no one knows where he is?'

'That is what I said.'

'Then what happened to him?'

'This I do not know.'

Utterson nodded. 'Then have you ever heard of a man called Henry Jekyll?'

'I have not.'

'Have you ever seen a man around here, tall, particularly handsome, thick black hair greying at the temples, bronze complexion?'

'This description means nothing to me.'

'Then would you be so good as to contact me at my chambers, should he appear at any stage? Or if Dr. Preiss returns?'

The man agreed, without much conviction, and Utterson gave him a note bearing his firm's Bedford Row address.

Utterson then remembered Jekyll's dentist, a certain Dr. Bennett in Great Ormond Street, and he remembered also the peerless condition of Jekyll's gums, and how, in certain recent cases—when a body was burned beyond recognition, for instance—dental records had furnished the only means of identification. Was it possible, then, that Bennett might expose the impostor simply by examining the man's maw?

But Bennett's residence, when Utterson found it, was like a gap in a row of perfectly maintained teeth.

'Burned to ciders,' one of the neighbours told him, strolling past with a feisty terrier. 'Along with everything inside.'

'And Dr. Bennett as well?'

'Poor sod,' the neighbour said, nodding. 'Sleeping at the time, he was. Left a fire roaring in the hearth and the cinders set fire to the rug—or so they say.'

'When did this happen?'

'Two months ago, or thereabouts.'

Utterson surveyed the blackened ruins. 'There were no suspicious circumstances?'

'Not that I know of.'

'And what about his papers—his dental records?'

'Have a look,' the neighbour said, with the dog straining on its leash. 'If wood and plaster failed to survive, then what chance would you give a man's records?'

It occurred to Utterson that there was still another in London who had known Henry Jekyll even more intimately than his doctors. Moreover, the widow Spratling had a vested interest in clearing the matter up as efficiently as possible. But how could he bring the claimant before her? And how, for that matter, would he convince the impostor to submit to her examinations? He decided to visit her anyway, if only for the excuse of enjoying her company again.

When he arrived at her street in Shepherd's Bush, however, he was surprised to find Terrence standing dumbly on the corner.

'Good afternoon, Terrence—are you supposed to be out?'

The boy had his hands buried deep in his pockets and was staring fixedly across the street, where some half-dressed girls were skipping rope: '*Two little dickie birds sitting on a wall, one named Peter, the other named Paul.*'

'Come with me,' Utterson said, but when he extended his hand Terrence shook him off brusquely.

'Very well,' said Utterson, frowning. 'I shall consult with your mother.'

Terrence, still watching the girls, was eerily silent.

Perturbed, Utterson continued to the widow's door, upon which he knocked with his jackal-headed cane. But for a long time there was no response.

'*One bright and pretty, the other dark and small . . .*'

He was about to turn back to Terrence, seeking an explanation, when the door flew open.

The widow Spratling, looking as though she had just tumbled out of bed, was dragging a shawl over her shoulders.

'Gabriel!' she exclaimed. 'I thought it was Terrence!'

'May I have a word with you inside, Nora?' Utterson asked—the noise from the neighbouring bone-grinding works, not to mention the trilling of the skipping girls, was grating on his nerves.

'One full of feathers, one with none at all . . .'

The widow hesitated, her hand still tight on the door.

'I shan't be long,' Utterson assured her, then took the liberty of stepping into the musty passage. 'I certainly don't mean to bother you,' he said, removing his hat. 'It's just that the impostor I've mentioned to you, the fraudster claiming to be Henry Jekyll, has been going around—'

He was interrupted by the sound of footsteps. Boards creaking like ship timbers. And then a cheerful, terribly familiar voice:

'Utterson! Good Lord, man—can I not get away from you?'

Utterson, seized with dread, looked up. And saw, standing at the top of the stairs, the Jekyll claimant himself, stuffing his shirttails into his trousers.

'Just like old times, eh?'

Utterson, shrunk to the size of pin, turned to the widow, whose eyes were downcast, then back to the claimant, who was smiling wolfishly.

'Why not come join us, old chap? Good times for all, what?'

Starved of air, Utterson span around and stormed into the street, where even Terrence had an impish gleam in his eye.

'A wicked wench, is your mama . . .' the boy said, in a mocking old man's voice, and Utterson stared at him until he could bear it no more.

Then he took off in the direction of the city, fleeing the scene like a biblical catastrophe, and wondering, fleetingly, if he might really have lost his mind.

'*Fly away Peter, fly away Paul; don't come back till the heavens fall.*'

A Conspicious Absence

ORCED INTO UNEXPECTED detours by roadworks and bridge building, Utterson by the time he reached Gaunt Street had regained enough composure to order Poole into the drawing room.

'There's something I need to show to you, Poole,' he announced in a strained voice. 'A statement, written by your former master.'

'By Dr. Jekyll?' Poole asked, frowning.

'That's right.'

'So you have seen him since . . . our meeting?'

'What? No, no, *not him*. Not the impostor, for heaven's sake. I mean a statement written by the *real* Henry Jekyll. A statement I collected from the dissecting rooms on that terrible night we found Hyde dead—you must remember it.'

Poole looked puzzled. 'I recollect a document . . .'

'A statement,' said Utterson. 'I brought it back here to read before returning to Jekyll's home, where we summoned the police.'

Poole nodded. 'Instructions as to property and bank accounts . . .'

'I beg your pardon?'

'You said the document contained instructions relating to property and bank accounts.'

Utterson nodded impatiently. 'Yes, that's what I said at the time. But I lied to you, Poole. I was trying to protect your master, and did not want to sully the name of a good friend.'

Poole's brow furrowed.

'The statement was shocking,' Utterson explained. 'Unspeakable. I read it just two or three times, yet it has festered in my mind ever since. And now, provided you feel capable of taking in its content, I wish to show it to you.'

'You retained this document?'

'In my safe upstairs. With a corroborating statement by Hastie Lanyon, which you must also read.'

'If you insist, sir.'

'It is not a matter of insisting. You must *want* to know the truth. And keep in mind you will very probably be appalled. Your faith in many things will be tested. But it is in your best interests, whether you know it or not. Are you ready?'

'I suppose so, sir.'

Utterson ascended the stairs to his business room, where he opened his safe—with unexpected difficulty—and reached for the innermost compartment. He felt around but the compartment seemed empty. He leaned in for a closer examination. No statements. He foraged in some other compartments, opened a few folders, but nothing. A wave of panic surged through him and slowly ebbed.

There was no need to be alarmed. The statements were in the safe somewhere, they had to be. He vividly remembered locking them away on that ghastly night, just as he remembered seeing them several times in the years after that.

So he searched every compartment again. He opened every box. He transferred everything to his desk—wills, deeds, keepsakes—and laid it all out. He combed through it all exhaustively. It took him close to half an hour, yet he still could find no statement by Henry Jekyll, and no corroborating narrative by Hastie Lanyon.

'Will sir be requiring dinner?'

With a jolt Utterson became aware of his butler standing primly at the door. 'What?' he snapped.

'Will sir be requiring dinner?' Poole asked, eyebrows arched.

Utterson sensed mockery. '*You* took them, I suppose.'

'Sir?'

'You opened the safe and removed the statements, did you?'

'Sir?'

'Did he order you to do it? The impostor? Did he tell you to destroy them?'

Poole looked aggrieved. 'Are you suggesting that I stole something from your safe, sir?'

'Well, did you?'

'Sir,' the butler said, gulping, 'you must know that I would never do such a thing. You must know that I *could* never do such a thing.'

'Oh yes?' Utterson said, but could not challenge Poole's manifest sincerity. 'Well, the fact remains that this safe has been broken into. And some very important documents have been removed. There is no doubt about it, none at all. So what explanation can there be?'

The butler tried to be helpful. 'Is it not possible,' he suggested, 'that you removed the documents yourself?'

'Of course not!' Utterson said. 'Do you think I would not remember if I had?' Then a thought occurred to him. 'Last night,' he said, 'last night . . . at the impostor's dinner, I mentioned the statements . . . I even mentioned that they were safely stored. And now that I think of it . . . yes, that's right'—he looked at Poole—'you said there were noises in the house last night, did you not?'

'I heard you moving about, sir.'

'Yes, but what makes you think it was me? Did you see me? Did you actually see me?'

'No, sir.'

'Then why would it be me? I was sleeping like a bear. So why would I be moving around the house?'

'You might have been sleepwalking, sir.'

'Sleepwalking?'

'You've done it before, sir.'

'Sleepwalk! Me?'

'Aye, sir. You often walk around the house at night. You crash into walls and throw things on the floor, and mumble oaths.'

'I throw things!'

'In your sleep, sir.'

Utterson felt chilled. 'And how long has this been going on?'

'Since as long as I've been here.'

'And why have you never bothered to mention it before?'

'I thought it might embarrass you, sir.'

'Embarrass me!' Utterson felt stricken. 'But . . .'

But he was tongue-tied.

'Begging your pardon, sir,' Poole ventured, 'but do you think that might be the explanation? That you sleepwalked into the business room and opened the safe, and disposed of the documents in a daze?'

'Yes . . .' Utterson could see that Poole was offering a charitable solution, but under the circumstances it would have to suffice. 'Yes, that must be it. Thank you, Poole, thank you. You may continue preparing dinner.'

He collected all his papers and stuffed them back into his safe, then closed the door tightly and keyed the locks. But all the time he was wondering how he could possibly be certain of anything, if he was no longer certain of himself.

A Mist Dispersed

IN THE MORNING Utterson arrived early at his desk, set out his inks, laid out a sheaf of legal paper, and as meticulously as possible, with a furiously scratching pen, began reconstructing Henry Jekyll's full statement of the case.

Words, sentences, whole paragraphs knitted together with astonishing clarity—almost as if Utterson himself had composed them:

The worst of my faults was a certain impatient gaiety, a profound duplicity . . . those provinces of good and ill which divide and compound man's dual nature . . . I managed to compound a drug . . . I knew I risked death . . . any drug that so potently shook the very fortress of identity . . .

Utterson, his tongue poking catlike from his lips, grew more and more excited as he filled page after page. Because he recognised Jekyll's distinctive voice in everything he wrote:

I watched them boil and smoke . . . I drank off the potion . . . the most racking pains, a grinding of the bones, deadly nausea . . . I came to myself as if out of a great sickness . . . I knew myself to be more wicked, tenfold more wicked . . . I was aware that I was smaller, lighter and younger than Henry Jekyll . . . Edward Hyde was pure evil.

Occasionally, it was true, Utterson's hand faltered a little, even stopped writing altogether; because the meaning of these words, seen starkly on paper, was undeniably strange: that a man could imbibe a potion and change into a different being? That he could shrink in height and become unrecognisable even to his closest friends? This certainly was not something that could be brought confidently before a court.

The drug shook the prison-house of my disposition . . . my evil was swift to seize the occasion . . . the pleasure began to turn towards the monstrous . . . my devil had long been caged, and came out roaring . . . a furious propensity to ill . . . the spirit of hell awoke in me and raged . . . a mist dispersed . . . a divided ecstasy of mind . . .

But now Utterson's hand had quickened again, because the confession was written with such manifest sincerity that it was beyond the realms of fiction; and he, being a lawyer, was something of an expert in the mendacity of criminals. So this statement simply had to be true. It *had* to be.

Will Hyde die upon the scaffold? Or will he find the courage to release himself at the last minute? God knows; I am careless; this is the true hour of my death, and what is to follow concerns another than myself. Here then, as I lay down the pen, and proceed to seal up my confession, I bring the life of the unhappy Henry Jekyll to an end.

By now the office around him had filled with noise and bustle. Entirely oblivious, Utterson drew out a new sheaf of papers and started recreating the second document—Hastie Lanyon's account of Hyde's transformation back into Jekyll.

Twelve o'clock had scarce rung out over London when the knocker sounded . . . I found a small man crouching on the portico . . . he had a shocking expression on his face . . . his clothes were enormously too large for him . . . something abnormal and misbegotten in his very essence . . . 'Have you got it?' he cried . . . 'This is it, sir,' I said . . . a phial full of blood-red liquor, highly pungent . . . he sprang to it . . . he put the glass to his lips, and drank at one gulp . . . he seemed to swell . . . the features seemed to melt and alter . . . 'Oh God!' I screamed . . . for there before my eyes stood Henry Jekyll!

It was true, the voice in Lanyon's letter—the syntax and the idioms—seemed remarkably similar to that of the first letter, the one composed by Henry Jekyll; but surely that should be no surprise, as Jekyll and Lanyon had known each other since Cambridge and circulated in the same galaxy afterwards. It was also to be admitted that Lanyon had mixed his dates at one point—claiming to have received written instructions from Jekyll both in January and several weeks earlier—but then, as Utterson knew, every man's memory plays tricks on him occasionally. So in the end he was able to look at the two reconstructed documents with a great sense of personal achievement. He had certainly convinced himself, if he had convinced no other. And he was not losing his mind.

He summoned his head clerk.

'Do you have a safe in your home, Mr. Guest?'

'I'm afraid not, sir.'

'Then a hiding place of some sort? Somewhere that you might store valuables?'

'I can easily find one.'

Utterson made a noise of approval. 'Over seven years ago my dear friend Hastie Lanyon charged me with the responsibility of storing a letter in his name, and opening it only upon his disappearance. Now, Mr. Guest, I am charging *you* with the task of secreting these two documents you see before you, and open-ing them only upon *my* disappearance. Do you think you are up to it?'

'I suppose so, sir,' Guest said, and frowned. 'But may I enquire, sir, about the substance of the documents?'

'They are statements relating to the crimes of Henry Jekyll—and that is all you need to know for now.' Utterson passed them over. 'Take them and show them to no one.'

'Are you heading out, sir?' Guest asked, for the lawyer was reaching for his cane.

'I am—why?'

'Mr. Spurlock is here to see you again.'

Utterson waved dismissively. 'Mr. Slaughter can see him.'

'Mr. Slaughter has a full schedule this morning, and Mr. Spurlock has already been waiting for some time, sir.'

'Very well,' replied Utterson, annoyed. 'I shall see him, but no one else after that. Has there been any correspondence from Mr. Enfield, by the way?'

'Nothing, sir; and nothing from the gentleman you engaged to look into it. Are you intending to attend the funeral of Sir Palfrey Bramble?'

'I beg your pardon?'

'Sir Palfrey Bramble—it was in the papers, sir. He passed away in his bed on Friday night.'

'Sir Palfrey? Are you certain?'

'Certain as taxes, sir.'

Utterson remembered calling on the florid-faced explorer just a few days earlier; and now the man—corpulent, excitable, permanently flushed—was dead. It was one of those passings that evoke sadness but little surprise.

'Well, that is sobering news indeed,' said Utterson, without any real inclination to dwell on it. 'In any case . . . send in Mr. Spurlock.'

Hudson Spurlock, dressed in all the colours of a harlequin, masqueraded as an importer of Persian finery but was widely known around town as a master thief. From his headquarters in the public houses around the Elephant and Castle he presided over a small army of swindlers, pickpockets, forgers and safe-crackers, whom he daily dispatched to all corners of the city. His business with Utterson & Slaughter related strictly to some small claims cases, but as Utterson listened distractedly—Spurlock had been sued by a building contractor for failing to meet his debts—a rogue thought occurred to him.

'Never mind about that,' he said suddenly.

'Never mind—?'

'About your debts, Mr. Spurlock. I shall see to it that the case is prolonged indefinitely, and our services rendered at half—no, a quarter—of the customary fee.'

Spurlock blinked. 'Very generous of you, Mr. Utterson, but you will forgive me for—'

'By way of apology on my part, for keeping you waiting this morning, and failing to attend to you last week.'

'Very gracious indeed.' Spurlock fluffed the point of his beard. 'And yet—and you will still forgive me for saying so—I'm not sure that the sins in this case warrant the penance.'

Utterson grunted. 'You think my goodwill comes at a price?'

'Just my naturally suspicious disposition, Mr. Utterson.'

'Then your disposition does not deceive you, Mr. Spurlock.'

Spurlock's smile showed a glint of gold. 'You wish to draw upon my special skills, perhaps?'

'A small favour, and time is of the essence.'

'Then I am happy to be of assistance, Mr. Utterson—as long as it does not take me too far out of my way.'

'By no means—it is very close to your base of operations, in fact.'

An hour later they were in Utterson's Gaunt Street business room, inspecting the lawyer's safe.

'In truth I cannot say,' the thief admitted. 'There's some scoring around the tumblers, to be sure, but the locks are aged to begin with.'

'Still, they *could* have been picked?'

'Do you keep the keys with you?'

'At all times.'

'Then it's possible—if you were deep asleep, or passed out from drinking—that they might be lifted from you. Or the locks could have been twirled with the very best equipment. But still . . .'

'Still . . .?'

'It would need to be a master, Mr. Utterson, and there's not a soul in this town as skilled as me.'

'That you know of.'

'I know most of 'em.'

'But not all.'

'No, not all.'

'Then the fact remains—the safe could have been sprung, yes?'

Spurlock sniffed and smiled at the same time. 'If that's what you wish to hear, Mr. Utterson, then I'm happy enough to say it.'

Utterson ruminated for a moment, then looked again at the thief.

'How would you like a completely clean bill, Mr. Spurlock?'

'A *completely* clean bill, Mr. Utterson?'

'No charges for services rendered by me—not now, and not ever again.'

The sparkle in Spurlock's eye matched that of his tooth. 'And what, if I might ask, is the price of your charity now, Mr. Utterson?'

The lawyer sighed but did not answer directly. 'Can I call upon you tonight? Around midnight? Can I do that, Mr. Spurlock?'

The Darkness of the Dissecting Rooms

A STOREHOUSE OF INDIAN tea near the river had caught fire, the air was filled with fragrant smoke, and flurries of roasted tealeaves, like clouds of black pollen, were settling on every projection.

Hudson Spurlock, looking remarkably at home in a filthy broadcloth tunic and moleskins, had already warned Utterson he would not be lingering after the job was done: 'I've got no love for Newgate,' he said. The two men were lurking in shadows across the square from the Jekyll home, waiting for the house lights to dim, retreating deep into the darkness whenever constables appeared, peeking out whenever it was safe, puffing, stamping, and waving away the thickening drizzles of aromatic ash. But it was not until midnight that the last light in the place was extinguished, and even then Spurlock did not move at once.

'A thief's most important tool is patience,' he whispered.

So Utterson, decidedly impatient, committed himself to further waiting. In fact, he was not even sure what he was going to do once inside the Jekyll home, but the need to find incriminating evidence—anything at all—had become overpowering. That very afternoon he had received a letter from the widow Spratling that seemed the final straw:

My Dearest Angel,

You must not think the worst of me, because things are not always as they seem. When the man calling himself Henry Jekyll arrived at my home yesterday, Terrence had left on an errand and the visitor suffered a fainting fit owing he said to his constricting clothes. He was loosening these articles upstairs and I was changing into something more presentable, in order to receive him in an appropriate manner, when you appeared at the door. I must say I am still unable to determine if the man is really Henry Jekyll or an impostor as you have claimed, so I have consented to another meeting with him, during which I intend to examine him more closely.

Your most faithful friend,
Nora

Utterson had enough experience with Bathshebas and even Jezebels to recognise a woman who was testing the shoals in a shifting stream. Nevertheless he was prepared to forgive Nora everything, all her chicanery, as long as he emerged victorious in the end. Indeed, he decided she would become even more desirable once he had accounted for the claimant—once the dragon had been slain by the angel.

'Time enough,' Spurlock decided suddenly. 'Wait here awhile, Mr. Utterson, and keep a sharp eye out for peelers.'

Emerging from his reverie, Utterson watched as Spurlock ambled casually up the by-street, looking left and right, and drawing from his pocket a ring of rough-edged keys. Then, at the door of the dissecting rooms, the thief dropped to one knee and began inserting these blanks in the lock, testing each before settling on one that offered the most promise. This he started filing industriously as Utterson watched from afar.

There was an explosion in the distance and the gas lamps fluttered like startled spirits.

'Evenin' there, sir.'

Utterson was startled—he had noticed no approach—but quickly drew himself together. 'Oh, hullo there, constable.'

'Waitin' for someone?'

'A companion of mine,' Utterson managed. 'We were forced to make a detour because of the fire.'

The portly PC, who bore a Yorkshire accent, looked up at the reddened clouds. 'So you've been in the vicinity of the fire, have you?'

'A most distressing sight.'

'Reached the fish market yet, has it?'

Utterson, doing his best not to look in Spurlock's direction, nodded distractedly. 'Yes, the . . . I mean, the fish market?'

'Billingsgate Market.'

'Yes, I . . . I don't know. It might have.'

The PC looked him up and down. 'Not from this part of town, are you?'

'Passing through, you know. From the south.'

'South London?'

'Suffolk.'

'I'm from York originally.'

'Fancy that.'

'Well, good night to you then, sir.'

'And to you, constable.'

Utterson waited until the PC had waddled on, testing shutter-bolts and door-handles, before looking again up the by-street. But suddenly Spurlock was nowhere to be seen. Panicking, he crept over to the dissecting rooms, looking frantically in every direction, but there was no sign of the thief anywhere. Then he heard a hiss from the adjoining courtyard and the thief, to his relief, came out of the shadows.

'All done,' Spurlock announced.

'The door?'

'See for yourself.'

Utterson turned, saw the door was slightly ajar, and nodded with satisfaction. 'Then I shall see you again in Bedford Row, Mr. Spurlock?'

'When I need some services rendered,' Spurlock said, 'you will.' The thief flashed his tooth and dissolved again into the darkness.

Alone, Utterson extended a hand to the hideous door, pushed it open by degrees and, with a sharp intake of breath, stepped through. The room was as dark as a crypt. There was a powerful odour of furniture polish and disturbed dust. He stood motionless for a good minute, simply reacquainting himself with the building's abrasive spirit—this was, after all, where Jekyll had conducted his dreadful experiments—then struck a match, lit his bull's-eye lantern and proceeded warily across the floor.

Almost immediately he tripped over a protuberance and fell in a clattering heap.

When he picked up the lantern, which was flaring wildly, he saw that his foot had snagged on the curled leg of a statue—a Hindoo statue, like something belonging to Sir Palfrey Bramble. In fact, now that he raised the lamp and directed its light about the chamber, he saw numerous other treasures arranged around the room, along with many other articles concealed under dustsheets.

He was lifting the hem of one of these robes—he saw a tantalising glimpse of a Louis Quinze lampstand—when there was a shuffling sound and the grinding of a key in the lock.

Someone was entering the rooms from the other side!

Swiftly Utterson extinguished the lantern and stumbled backwards. He reached the street just as the opposing door creaked open. He fell outside onto the pavement, eased the blistered door closed and whisked across to the refuge of an alleyway.

Panting, pressed back against the bricks, he watched as the dissecting rooms opened and the sooty little fellow with the odious face, together with the brutish butler called Baxter, slipped out into the gaslight. The two men looked around with no exceptional caution—clearly they hadn't noticed him—and then padded down the by-street, heading purposefully into the night.

Fortifying himself with a few lungfuls of tea-stained air, Utterson consulted his pocket watch—it was already one o'clock—and resolved to follow them to hell and back if necessary, for he could tell that they were bent on infamy.

A Hellish Glow

UTTERSON STALKED THE men foxlike for twenty minutes. When they rounded corners he hastened forward, fearing he might lose sight of them; when they took straight pathways he reverted to a comfortable distance; and whenever they gave any indication that they might turn around he ducked with alacrity into the nearest alcove. But the two men seemed oblivious of his presence, chatting freely, looking up at the hellish clouds, kicking sometimes at refuse on the pavement, the smaller man shuffling along in a manner that to Utterson seemed eerily reminiscent of Mr. Hyde.

In fact, now that he considered it at length, was it not conceivable that the claimant *was* transforming himself into a different being? Though Utterson had long ago secreted all Jekyll's recorded formulae, was it not possible that something—a single page, perhaps—had been left behind in the Jekyll house, or unearthed somewhere during the impostor's research? And if that were the case, was it not possible that the claimant had taken advantage of the potion to pursue his sinister agenda—a man in disguise hiding beneath yet another disguise?

'Dr. Guise indeed,' Utterson mused under his breath.

But no sooner had these words escaped his lips than he lost sight of his quarries entirely. A fire cart came careering up the street, the horses whipped to a frenzy, the fireman rattling a bell, and Utterson squeezed against some church railings to allow it a clear passage. But when the vehicle had gone, leaving in its wake a trail of disturbed air, he found to his horror that the two men had vanished.

He sped around the corner and looked in every direction; he selected a path on impulse and followed it for three blocks, peering into every ill-lighted alley; he turned back; he headed in frantic circles; but he could see them nowhere.

Presently he found himself in Cavendish Square, the neighbourhood of Chauncey Wiseman and Edmond Keyes among others—and suddenly a chilling possibility occurred to him.

For he had followed the two men expecting them to arrive at some dark door—a smuggler's warehouse, perhaps, or a bandit's bolthole—but if their destination were the environs of Cavendish Square, then what did that say about their intentions? What business could they have in a respectable neighbourhood such as this?

Utterson vacillated awhile, fragrant cinders raining around him, before deciding his only recourse was to call for assistance. But when he entered the nearest police station, which was two blocks away, he found the portly PC from Yorkshire, the same one he had encountered outside the Jekyll home, standing in the entrance hall brushing ash off his uniform.

'Oh, hullo again, sir—did you find your companion?'

Utterson tightened. 'I . . . I'm terribly sorry, sir. I mistook this place for . . .' But inspiration deserted him and he backed awkwardly out of the door, stumbling over his heels and toppling into the street.

He resumed his patrol of the neighbourhood, hoping to apprehend the two culprits as they emerged, blood-stained perhaps, from some well-to-do residence. But clearly he could not continue going around in circles without a convincing explanation to offer to the police. So he headed back to Jekyll's square and concealed himself again like a cricket in a crack, intending to confront the two suspects upon their return. But hours elapsed, milk drays and market gardeners' carts started to appear, and he became increasingly despondent and fatigued.

He was not even sure how he returned home, if indeed he returned home at all, for when he awoke he was sprawled over his office desk in Bedford Row, glued to the blotter by his own slobber. Someone was tapping him on the shoulder.

'Utterson, dear fellow'—it was Mr. Slaughter—'we really must have a word about this. In private, if you please.'

Gideon Slaughter, a glowing cherub of a man with carrot-coloured hair, was plainly both daunted and excited by the prospect of upbraiding the firm's senior partner. In his magisterial office, filled with Olympian furniture, he installed himself behind his desk and nervously set to polishing his pocket watch.

'I know we all have times when we are not functioning at our best,' he began, 'but if you really are as ill as you seem, dear Utterson, do you not think it might be best if you had some rest?'

'I am not ill,' Utterson assured him. 'There's some urgent business I've been attending to, that's all.'

'Relating to the Jekyll estate.'

'That is correct.'

Slaughter's watch-polishing became even more furious. 'You know,' he said, 'though it's none of my business, naturally, I wonder if you should let these events take their proper course. I mean to say, if this claimant fellow really is who he says he is, then do you not think it might be better to let him establish his bona fides and offer him any assistance he needs?'

Utterson felt betrayed. 'To whom have you been talking about this?'

Slaughter began winding the watch. 'Now, now, I have ears, Utterson, I have—'

'It was Mr. Guest, was it?'

'No, it was not Guest.'

'Then who?'

Slaughter was still winding. 'Well, there's no danger in telling you, I suppose. It was that inspector fellow, the one who—'

'Newcomen?' Utterson said. 'Inspector Newcomen was here?'

'He was. He—'

'What on earth did he want?'

'He was just making a few enquiries. Clearing up a few things.'

'*Clearing up* a few things . . .!' Utterson stared into middle-space.

'The point is, dear fellow,' Slaughter said, snapping the watch shut, 'that the man calling himself Jekyll seems unusually well-credentialed for a so-called impostor. It seems he's already convinced many of his old friends, been pledged numerous endorsements, and even secured some substantial loans to tide him over. So don't you think, old boy, that it might be better to see how it all plays out?'

A Hellish Glow

'*Old boy?*' said Utterson.

Slaughter reddened. 'What I mean to say is . . . well, don't you think it might be better for your health, not to mention your peace of mind, if you were to surrender some of your ambitions? None of us lives for ever, do we? I mean to say, look at what happened to Palfrey Bramble and Edmond Keyes, for heaven's sake.'

'Edmond Keyes?'

'The professor of ancient history.'

'Yes, damn it, I know what he is—what about him?'

Slaughter slid his watch into a pocket. 'Dear Utterson—do you mean to say you've not heard?'

'Heard what? *What?*'

'Well,' Slaughter went on uncomfortably, 'Professor Keyes fell down his stairs in the middle of the night and cracked his head open on a banister. Died instantaneously, poor chap. I say—!'

But he did not get a chance to finish, because Utterson was already flashing through the door.

133

The Fortress of Identity

L ET ME SEE if I can follow what you are now telling me,' Newcomen said, leaning back in his chair. 'Two men in the employ of Dr. Jekyll are thieves and murderers, sent out by night to do his bidding. You say they dispose of gentlemen who might know too much about their master's real identity, and therefore have become too much of a threat; and meanwhile they ransack the homes of the same gentlemen, in order to claim a bounty of stolen treasures.'

Utterson nodded. 'Consider the evidence,' he said. 'Jekyll's half-brother—a man who conceivably furnished crucial information to the claimant—is now dead. Jekyll's doctor at the time of his disappearance—a man who might have identified him physically—is missing. His dentist—a man who might have recognised him by his teeth alone—is also dead, and his records put to flame. And most recently, in the last few days, Sir Palfrey Bramble and Edmond Keyes, two of Jekyll's closest friends, have died as well.'

Newcomen grunted. 'And yet all these deaths have been thoroughly investigated and all suspicious circumstances discounted. Nor were any valuables missing from their premises.'

'But can you really attest to that?' Utterson argued. 'Really attest?'

'I would have heard had there been any improprieties.'

'But surely the investigations into Bramble and Keyes are not already closed?'

'Sir Palfrey died in his sleep. Edmond Keyes, as far as I know, died as the result of a common accident.'

'Then would you be interested to hear that the two brutes of whom I speak, the ones in the impostor's employ, were seen in the vicinity of Keyes's residence last night?'

'Seen by whom?' Newcomen asked. 'By you?'

Utterson coughed. 'By someone I know in Cavendish Square.'

'Hmph,' Newcomen said. 'I can't see it makes any difference, in any event—Keyes died on Sunday morning, many hours before whatever you or anyone else may have seen last night.'

Utterson managed to recover quickly from his surprise. 'And then there is the simple application of logic,' he went on. 'Consider the mathematical probability of such a coincidence—that such a large number of men in Jekyll's circle would all die within a matter of months.'

'I'm a policeman, Utterson—I have been for eighteen years. And I fancy I know a fair bit about mathematical probabilities.'

'Not to mention the small matter of the claimant's bounty,' Utterson tried. 'All those treasures in the dissecting rooms, I mean—they must have come from somewhere.'

'Well, the doctor has been away for some years, and would very likely have accumulated a few souvenirs in that time. Besides, how do *you* know what's in his dissecting rooms?'

'I . . . I heard someone talking at the dinner,' Utterson said.

'Who?'

'I can't remember.'

Newcomen looked doubtful. 'You've not been doing anything foolish, I hope?'

'But surely you see what the impostor is doing?' Utterson went on. 'Under the pretence of visiting old friends he cases out their homes and then sends his hounds in to plunder their valuables. And silence the occupants, too, should they stumble upon the crime.'

'Minutes ago you were saying that the victims were murdered for knowing too much about Jekyll,' the inspector said. 'Now you say they were killed because they stumbled upon a theft in progress?'

'One or the other, it makes no difference,' Utterson insisted. 'And there's one other thing, Inspector. One other thing. You are free to disbelieve me when I say this, but I have good reason to suspect that the smaller thief, the little man with the odious face, is in fact the claimant in disguise. This could be the way he goes about his murderous enterprises undetected.'

'The little man is the claimant too?'

'That's right.'

'Dr. Jekyll?'

'The man claiming to be Jekyll—he could be.'

Newcomen snorted. 'This is getting rather fantastic, Utt—'

'I know what it sounds like,' Utterson interrupted. 'I *know*. But surely it cannot hurt to investigate with an open mind? As a favour to a man who, I think I can say without conceit, has a reputation for being the least excitable lawyer in London.'

'Least excitable, are you?'

'Have you reason to contest the point?'

Newcomen seemed on the verge of saying something but settled on shaking his head. 'Very well, Mr. Utterson,' he said.

'Then perhaps you can tell me what I can do to make you less excitable still?'

An hour or so later the two men were being led through the Jekyll home by the claimant himself. An encroaching storm was sending out salvoes of thunder, and the china in the kitchen, the mirrors in the passage, the brass before the fireplace—all were rattling to its tempo.

'I hope there's nothing wrong.' The claimant, fitted snugly in Jekyll's favourite smoking jacket, had his eyebrows knitted innocently.

'Just a small matter,' Newcomen assured him, 'that needs to be cleared up.'

Utterson, irritated, was more forthright. 'Where were you last night, sir—can you answer that?'

'Last night?' The claimant's brow furrowed further. 'Why do you ask, dear Utterson?'

'Were you out on the streets, by any chance?'

'As it happens I was visiting our mutual friend Christopher Piggott—as you can verify with Piggott himself.'

'And after that? When you returned home?'

'I retired to bed, naturally.'

'Did you? Really?'

'I don't suppose I can prove it to you, Utterson, if you are intent on disbelieving everything I say.'

Utterson scowled. 'And where pray tell was Mr. Butler?'

'Mr. Butler?'

'Mr. Baxter. Your butler. You know who I mean.'

'Baxter? You weren't following him, I hope.'

'That's not an answer.'

'Well, I hate to disappoint you, but Mr. Baxter was fetching some supplies for my next dinner.'

'Supplies for your dinner, eh?'

'Pork, mainly. There's a slaughterhouse, Ogden's—he knows the foreman there.'

'He visits in *the middle of the night?*'

'Well, I don't ask too many questions. Back door, cough cough, look the other way, you know. I hope this doesn't upset you, Inspector.'

Newcomen shrugged. 'I've heard of such things.'

'Oh, yes,' Utterson chuckled. 'A slaughterhouse, you call it? Yes, it's a slaughterhouse, all right! But tell me, which of them does the slaughtering? Is it Baxter or the other one?'

'Other one?' By this time they had passed through the yard and arrived at the inner door to the dissecting rooms.

'The little fellow. The goblin. Who is he? Is he you?'

'Oh'—the claimant was inserting a key in the lock—'you've already met Eddie, have you?'

'*Eddie!*' It was Hyde's first name.

'My knife-boy.'

'A knife-boy now, is he?'

The claimant had now opened the door, and there, within the semi-darkness of the dissecting rooms, as if by some pre-arranged cue, was the hideous little man with the scorched and scoured countenance—'Eddie'—actually sharpening a knife on a stone.

'Speak of the devil,' the claimant said, faintly amused. 'Utterson here was just talking about you.'

'Nothing amiss, sir?' said the little man, scrunching his face.

'Nothing at all,' returned his master. 'Though I think, for the time being, you might be better off occupying yourself in the kitchen, old chap.'

'Cert'ly, sir.' With a tip of his cap, the little man—who smelled like an ill-tended fireplace—shuffled past and headed inside.

Utterson was taken aback by the casual *insolence* of it all—as though they were *mocking* him. But his distraction was not so great that he failed to notice, in the gloom of the dissecting rooms, the stolen articles still concealed under dustsheets. So it was on these that he now made an assault, lunging into the room and ripping off the first cover with a conjuror's flourish.

But there was nothing underneath apart from one of Jekyll's old vanity tables. Utterson tore off another sheet: a chest of drawers, also native to the Jekyll home. Another: an ornately carved ottoman. Utterson did not recognise it at first, and his heart leapt—but then he did.

Another. Another. Another.

In the end he exposed an entire gloomy chamber of disrobed furniture, but nowhere had he found a Hindoo sculpture, a Louis Quinze lampstand, or anything else he had glimpsed only the night before.

He looked up, blood pumping, and found the claimant and the inspector surveying him coolly.

'You've hidden them!' he spat at the claimant. 'You've hidden them somewhere else in the house!'

'Hidden, Utterson?'

'The bounty! The treasures you've stolen from the homes of others!'

'You're welcome to search through the whole place, if you so wish.'

The claimant had a glint in his eye; the inspector, by contrast, was visibly unimpressed; lightning was flashing through the cupola.

And suddenly a terrible conviction seized Utterson. 'You *saw* me last night, didn't you? You *knew* I was tracking your men! And you *knew* I was here as well—right here in this chamber!'

The claimant seemed perplexed. 'My dear fellow,' he said, 'I'm not even sure what you're suggesting . . .' He looked for assistance to Newcomen. 'Is he saying that he broke in here last night?'

'I hope not,' said Newcomen.

'Good Lord,' the claimant went on, frowning some more. 'But that doesn't bear thinking about. I mean, a man's home is his castle, his last refuge, his fortress.' He glanced at Utterson. 'The very fortress of his identity.'

Utterson gasped. '*The fortress* . . .!' He stared at the claimant wide-eyed; he gulped; he looked to the inspector; and he stabbed his finger accusingly. 'He's using Jekyll's words! From the statement!' he cried. '*He's using Henry Jekyll's words!*'

To which Inspector Newcomen exuded even more contempt, while the claimant himself offered a vaporous smile.

And Utterson, standing alone in the middle of the dissecting rooms, knew he had been dismantled—surgically cut apart. And he knew that he would forever be regarded as mad.

But he was not mad.

He was not!

Even if he was the only man in London who knew it.

The Keys of Hell and Death

MANY YEARS EARLIER Utterson had been a junior defence counsel representing Travis Hardwicke CIE, erstwhile district governor of the East India Company, after Hardwicke had been found alone with the body of Percy Sullivan, a rival businessman, in the rear of the company's club rooms in St James's Square. Sullivan's head had been bludgeoned; the weapon, a poker, was still in Hardwicke's grasp; Hardwicke himself was in a state of shock; and no one else was found in the vicinity. Notwithstanding the absence of any clear motive, it seemed an open and shut case of murder.

But when Hardwicke was interrogated by his legal team he insisted repeatedly and persuasively that he had acted in self-defence. He said that the victim had lured him to the deserted club with malicious intent; he said that Sullivan had for years been consumed by jealousy and ambition; he referred to the man's substantial history of fraud and misrepresentation; and he claimed that Sullivan had long been hounding him with threats and blackmail.

Hardwicke's command of detail was immaculate. He remembered incidents with astonishing precision; he never faltered or contradicted himself; and moreover he clearly believed everything he said.

And yet he was completely mad. In the Chancery his claims were swiftly put to the sword through evidence from former colleagues and disaffected relations. Hardwicke, it soon became clear, had been cultivating Sullivan as a nemesis for years, in order to project upon him all the sinister motives infecting his own heart; thus he had been able to fabricate events, memories and even documents while being blissfully unaware of his own part in the contrivance. He was, in effect, a divided self, unable to distinguish reality from his own fictions, and unconscious of his own actions even as he was performing them.

Though the case, a sensation in its day, had rapidly faded from the public memory, it had deeply impressed upon Utterson's mind the distorting power of the imagination. And as a consequence he had resolved never to be caught accepting any man's testimony without incontrovertible evidence (and even then to reserve an element of suspicion). It was through such means that he became renowned as a man uncorrupted by rashness or sentimentality—a grinding stone upon which others might file away their delusions.

And yet now Utterson had to ask if he himself was deluded. If his own grip on reality had loosened. If he needed to challenge his own identity.

Had he really gone insane?

But again and again, as many times as he prosecuted the case in his mind, he could not shake the foundations of his central convictions. The written statements of Henry Jekyll and Hastie Lanyon had really existed. Nor was he naturally given to fancies.

So everything in the documents was true. By drinking a potion Jekyll had transformed himself into Hyde. As Hyde, he had committed many unspeakable crimes. And he had killed himself in the body of Hyde.

Which meant that the claimant was an impostor. *He had to be.* There was simply no other explanation.

With his faith even firmer now that he had resisted a self-inflicted barrage, Utterson marched with renewed energy back to Gaunt Street, found the trunk containing Jekyll's receipts, and confronted Poole.

'You were the one who rounded up the powders and chemicals for Dr. Jekyll's potions, were you not?'

'Some of the time,' the butler admitted.

'Can you say from which chemist he drew his supplies? In the last year of his life especially?'

'If you mean before my master disappeared,' Poole said, 'there were a number of wholesalers he used, but in the main it was Maw & Co. of C— Street.'

'The one with the red and blue lanterns?'

'The same, sir.'

'Then prepare a light dinner, Poole, and I shall return, if all goes well, by eight o'clock.'

But at Maw & Co. he discovered that the man who customarily filled Jekyll's orders, a certain Mr. Halliday, had long since retired to Bethnal Green. Undaunted, Utterson took the train out to the old man's house.

The chemist, who was scarred of hands and caustic of personality, seemed bemused by the lawyer's questions.

'You're seeking what?'

'A recipe of Jekyll's, for a potion he mixed numerous times before his death.' Utterson handed across some of the doctor's orders.

'You think I can identify a potion by the ingredients alone?'

'I am relying on your assistance.'

'Jekyll was an odd one,' Halliday reflected. 'He asked for some queer combinations.'

'The potion I have in mind was particularly queer, giving off a pungent smell and a visible effervescence. Its effects were swift and dramatic.'

'Not saying it killed the doctor, are you?'

'Not directly, no.'

'Then why do you want it, precisely?'

Utterson sighed. 'I was Jekyll's lawyer and his dearest friend. I need to prove that the mixture in question had a conspicuous effect on his personality.'

'Not a bad thing if it did,' said Halliday, though he did not elaborate. Finally he peeled one of the receipts from Utterson's collection. 'I think this is the one you might be seeking.'

Utterson inspected the ingredients: phosphorous, ethanol, cocaine, psilocybe and other elements—indeed a peculiar mix.

'Jekyll spoke of a certain quantity of salt.'

'Possibly sodium chromate.'

'He suggested that this particular salt, which was essential to his formula, was impure.'

Halliday grunted. 'At Maw's we sold no impure salts. Perhaps he obtained it from elsewhere.'

'Might you know where?'

'Jekyll did not tell me everything.'

'Then do you have any idea how it might have become impure?'

'As I said to you, Jekyll ordered a great deal of sodium chromate—it yellowed his fingers. It might have become contaminated if it were stored in a vessel containing the residue of other powders. At any rate, that's the salt I'd be looking for if I were you.'

'Does Maw & Co. sell this salt, by any chance?'

'Of course,' said Halliday, 'but it would not be tainted, I tell you, unless their standards have fallen since my days.'

'Then I shall have to work with what they have.'

He hastened back to Maw & Co., rounded up the necessary supplies and hefted them in a crate to Gaunt Street, where his dinner was still simmering on the stove.

'Never mind that, Poole,' he said. 'Come upstairs with me.'

The butler dutifully followed his master to the business room, where Utterson laid out the various ingredients.

'Do you recognise these salts and tinctures?'

The butler looked uncertain.

'These are the same ingredients that Jekyll used in his last and most infamous experiment.'

'Sir?'

'That's right—and now I intend to mix them into a potion, in order to prove that a man is capable of transforming into another being, just as your former master turned himself into Edward Hyde.'

Poole blinked. 'My master . . . turned himself into Mr. Hyde?'

'Shocking, Poole, but true! That is the secret I have concealed from you for the last seven years. The man we found dead in the dissecting rooms that night was not just Mr. Hyde—it was Dr. Jekyll as well. And tonight, right here in this house, I shall prove it to you. I shall mix this potion in front of you, and I shall transform into another man!'

'Sir—'

'Doubt it all you like, Poole, but wait—wait and see!'

Swiftly he measured out his liquids and powders and mixed them together in a graduated glass, from whence issued vapours and odours. And when the concoction turned vivid purple, then vegetable green, just as Hastie Lanyon described in his state-ment, Utterson knew the compound was true.

'And now, Poole,' he said, hoisting the glass, 'you must bear witness to the folly of your former master. You must not avert your eyes; you must not shudder or recoil; above all you must use all your powers to prevent me from leaving this room, for I have in my hand the keys of hell and of death, and a monster inside me is about to be uncaged!'

'Sir—'

'Shut the door, Poole—and behold!'

And with that, Utterson tilted his head and in one gulp drained the contents of the foaming glass.

Mr. Utterson and Jericho Horn

THE POTION EXPLODED in Utterson's innards; his head ignited, his vision blurred; he convulsed, he struggled to breathe, he reached for his throat, he felt bile erupt; his eyes rolled, blood roared around his body, and his skin heated like a hot plate.

'Sir! Sir!' he heard Poole cry.

For a moment Utterson was convinced he was dying; he even wondered if he had just partaken of the same poison that had killed Mr. Hyde. And he recognised that this would be a just punishment for his folly, for being such a deluded, reckless, whimsical fool; so he surrendered; and the floor peeled away beneath him; and he collapsed onto a *chaise longue*; and his limbs slackened, and his body went limp; and his heart stilled; and he gave himself over to God.

There was blackness; and even more blackness.

But then something remarkable happened. As though in a dream Utterson saw his own body twitching and buckling; he saw Poole bending over him; he felt his whole body rearranging, he heard his bones grinding and bending, his muscles tighten and swell, his hair bristling like a wolf's, his bowels filling with foam, his knuckles cracking, his teeth sawing into his lips, and he tasted blood like an elixir in his throat.

'*Great God!*' exclaimed Poole, recoiling.

And Utterson, exulting, understood that he was not dead after all; he had reshaped himself; he had unleashed a demon within; and years of respectability had been torn away like a veil.

'Sir!'

This transformation, for Utterson, should have been enough. His intention, when mixing the potion, had been only to prove a possibility to both the butler and himself. But now, like Dr. Jekyll before him, he found himself intoxicated by a sense of freedom, of overwhelming recklessness—for all the walls of London were lined up before him, and they were crying out to be smashed.

He was no longer the angel Gabriel. He was Jericho Horn.

He snapped his eyes open and sprang to his feet, feeling stronger, leaner, sinewy, as taut as a coiled spring.

'You must *sit!*' Poole tried.

'Stand back, you ingrate!'

The voice, both guttural and forceful, rent the air like shrapnel; and only belatedly did Utterson realise, with surprise and delight, that it was his own.

'Sir—'

Utterson slammed the butler in the chest so hard that Poole toppled, grappling at the curtains before hitting the floor; and Utterson threw back his head and laughed.

'I should have done so years ago!' he cried, and spat hatefully at Poole before bustling out the door.

He capered down the stairs, seized his hat and cobra-headed cane—the hat slipped down around his temples, the cane felt like a truncheon—and tore open the door with wickedness in his heart and vengeance in his soul.

Heading up the street he found his tremendous energy and myriad thoughts could barely be contained in one body; so he jerked and jolted and snarled and chuckled; he loped and hunched and sprang and twisted from one side of the street to the other; he banged off lampposts and thumped off walls.

Passers-by shrank back and shielded themselves, for Utterson was like a ball of lightning in the shape of a man. 'Good evening, ladies,' he snarled, doffing his hat. 'And say how'd-you-do to Jericho Horn!'

As he approached the Thames his mind filled with the sound of bells and horns and sawing cellos, so that he imagined he was about to come upon some infernal orchestra, but then he understood he was not *smelling* the river but *hearing* it, because all his senses had been rearranged, and now smell had sound and sound had smell and colour had feeling—truly he had been born anew!

He did not pause for a single moment; he never faltered in his locomotive pace; he was an instrument of his bestial instincts; he charged headlong through bustling boulevards, curling streets and twisting lanes; he terrified rats and cats and cockroaches; he hissed in excitement as people around him dived for safety; and all the while the gas lights squealed, the air licked his face, colours reeked, the flagstones dazzled beneath his feet.

Finally he found himself outside the Jekyll home, where there were no lights in the windows; he hammered with the knocker and pounded the wood to no avail; he spun around and snarled at a cluster of curious onlookers—they wilted and ran—then rounded the corner to the dissecting rooms' entrance, where he found the knife-boy Eddie returning home with a bag of booty.

'Recognise me, do you?'

And when the scoundrel failed to respond Utterson seized him by the collar and flung him onto the cobbles, locking his hands around his throat and digging thumbnails through flesh.

'Where now is your master?'

Eddie squirmed and gasped as his eyeballs bulged; he struggled to say something, and Mr. Horn loosened his hands.

'Where is your master, I say?'

'At . . . at the theatre!'

'A surgical theatre?'

'A theatre . . . in the West End!'

'Which one?'

'D-don't'—Eddie sucked desperately at air—'don't know!'

Horn tossed the man aside and made off, shuffling, scrambling, gaining speed, his elbows pumping, his feet barely touching the ground; he giggled and cawed and hacked and hummed; and overheard lightning boomed and thunder flashed and oh, his senses reeled with the glory of it all, for inside him and out there was a tremendous storm.

In the theatre district the lights were sizzling as the crowds swarmed onto the streets amid a chaos of cabs and carriages; there were dowagers and stately gentlemen, men in court suits and gleaming top hats, ladies in plumes and furs and rustling silks.

Through all this Horn drove like a spear, gorging on his own distaste, thrilling at his revulsion; but everywhere his eyes darted he saw no sign of the claimant, nothing at all, until an odour invaded his nostrils and struck a switch in his brain; and then his nose, his eyes, his ears—all his senses in concert—told him he had picked up the stink of the impostor.

And there he was, the loathsome villain, made up like a Prussian horse guard, emerging from the Gaiety Theatre arm-in-arm with the widow Spratling—the duplicitous wench!— who in crimson bombazine looked as cheap as a cabbage-leaf cigar.

Horn felt his heart crashing, his brows bending; he heard the widow's lust like a mule driver's cry; and he drank of his own hatred as of a long-fermented wine.

Lightning snaked across the sky; rain slashed at the streets; the claimant and the widow ducked down a dimly lighted alley; and Horn himself hurtled after them, his blood so hot it was steaming through his skin. Halfway down, with water roiling and gurgling in the drainpipes, the claimant wheeled around with a look of reproach.

'Do I know you, sir?'

'You might know this!' cried Horn, and brought his cane flashing down on the man's nose; there was a crack of cartilage and a burst of blood. Horn struck again and again and again and again, a rain of bone-crunching blows, and the widow howled like a harpy.

Finally the impostor was on the floor of the alleyway, his life gushing into twinkling puddles and bloody Nora was pressed back against the bricks, with thunder growling, as Horn thrust his head into her face.

'Be I Gabriel now,' he cackled, 'or be I Lucifer?'

Then he lunged forward and tore the dress from her shoulders, so that her pink skin gleamed in the gaslight, and he seized her throat and stared into her eyes, fully prepared to take her like a tomcat.

But suddenly there was a whistle blast and he whirled around to see four constables flooding into the alley, and with one final grope at the fainting Nora he shot down the alley into Surrey Street and skittered down the darkest pathways to the embankment, taking many twists and turns until he had melted into the night.

The storm by now was fading but icy rain still cut through his clothes; he was heading swiftly to Gaunt Street with his bones grinding and rearranging, his muscles deflating, so that he sensed he was transforming back into the respectable lawyer of Bedford Row. And with that conviction a great shame seized him, and with every step he could scarce credit what diabolical powers had taken dominion of him. He shrank from the light and wept into the rain, filled not with desire but disgrace, and yearning for the consoling familiarity of his hearth.

At Gaunt Street, unable to find his key, he pounded on the door until Poole appeared and then Utterson dived into the hall where he stood dripping and bedraggled.

'I . . . I . . .' But he could not speak.

He raced up the stairway to his business room and sprawled across the *chaise longue* and sobbed into his hands until the darkness once more overcame him. And when he opened his eyes he found his butler standing over him with a searching look on his face.

'I smote him, Poole!' he exclaimed.

'You smote . . . who?'

'The impostor! The man calling himself Jekyll!'

'Faith!' Poole said. 'When?'

'Just now. But twenty minutes ago.'

'Twenty minutes ago!'

'In an alley off the Strand. Oh, why did you not obey me, Poole? When I ordered you not to allow me to leave this room?'

The butler was taken aback. 'But sir—'

'Oh, I know, Poole, it's my fault, of course it is! It's mine, for taking that infernal potion!'

'But sir—'

'None of this would have happened but for that formula. It ruined Jekyll and it has ruined me! What am I to do now, with blood on my hands?'

'But sir . . .' Poole licked his lips. 'I assure you, sir, you have not killed anyone.'

'But I did, Poole, you were not there to see!'

'But you did *not*, sir, I know it for certain.'

'You *cannot* know it, Poole.'

'But I *can*,' the butler insisted. 'Because *you have not left this room*, sir. After you drank from the glass you fell upon the sofa, twisting and shuddering, and drifting in and out of sleep.'

Utterson squinted incredulously. '*What?*'

'Sir, I promise you—you have been here in this room for at least an hour.'

Utterson shook his head. 'You lie . . . you must be lying!'

'Sir, I give you my bible-word.'

'But I was in the streets . . . I saw it all . . . I *felt* it all.'

'You tossed and moaned, sir, and you cried out, *but you did not leave this room.*'

161

Utterson prodded his shirtfront, which was damp. 'Then what about this rain on my clothes?'

'It is not rain, sir, but perspiration.'

'Perspiration!'

'You were very worked up, sir, and frothing at the mouth, as well.'

'Ahhh!' said Utterson, seeing for the first time that it might well be true. 'You mean I have not ventured out at all?'

'Not at all, sir.'

'Then I am not a killer after all?'

'Not that I know of, sir.'

'And the potion did not transform me?'

'It only made you writhe and sweat, sir.'

But now Utterson was faced with a prospect just as disagreeable as that of being a murderer—the appalling possibility that Jekyll's formula had never transformed anyone, and Jekyll was not Hyde.

Again shame and fear flooded over him.

'It was the impure salt!' he exclaimed.

'Sir?'

'The impure salt! Clearly the potion needs the impure salt!'

He stared at Poole, daring him to disagree. But Poole's expression, it seemed to him, had transformed from patronising pity into withering disdain.

Utterson bolted for the door.

The Burning Key

W ILD-EYED AND DISHEVELLED, Utterson spent much of the following morning visiting every pharmacy in a three-mile radius of the Jekyll home. But only a few could remember the doctor and none would admit to selling an impure salt. There was but one fragment of hope, when he learned of an elderly chemist named Enoch Fell who, not unlike Mr. Halliday, had completed some of the doctor's more eccentric orders. But unlike Mr. Halliday the whereabouts of Enoch Fell were unknown; it was even assumed that he had passed away. Utterson, vaguely aware of the intimidating effect his appearance was having on those he questioned, chuckled bleakly.

It was perversely amusing, in fact, the number of obstacles that were being strewn in his path—enough, certainly, to make the most rational man question his faculties. There were now just two days left until he should by rights assume full control of the Jekyll estate, and he was still the only man in London standing in the way of the impostor's designs.

Back at his office in Bedford Row he was unsurprised to discover that the claimant had now engaged the services of the highly credentialed solicitor Mr. Aubrey Bent, formally ending his association with Utterson & Slaughter.

'He thinks he's won,' Utterson breathed. 'He thinks he's already won this terrible game.'

'Game, sir?' said Guest.

Utterson snapped out of it. 'Never mind,' he said. 'Do you remember, by any chance, the recent death of Teddy Jekyll, Henry's half-brother?'

'Thomas Jekyll, sir.'

'I beg your pardon?'

'His name was Thomas Jekyll, sir. My name is Teddy.'

'Of course,' Utterson said. 'Nonetheless, I want you to find for me the firm that handled his affairs.'

'It was Kemp & Beatty of Essex Street, sir.'

'What's that?'

'I remember very well, sir, because I followed everything to do with Dr. Jekyll very closely—even the affairs of his half-brother.'

'You did, did you?' Utterson should not have been surprised—Guest was like a magpie with insignificant details—but he could not help but suspect some sinister motive. 'In any event, that's where I'm heading now—to Kemp & Beatty. Whether they're ready for me or not.' He picked up his hat.

'But what about the—'

'I don't care about . . . whatever it is. Slaughter can take care of it.'

'Mr. Slaughter, if I may say so, sir, is very concerned—'

'Slaughter can go to blazes!' Utterson spat. 'If I do not go there first!'

Utterson had time to register his clerk's look of alarm, even astonishment, before hastening down the back stairs. But here, by unhappy coincidence, he chanced across Mr. Slaughter himself, emerging from the water closet.

'Ah, Mr. Utterson,' said the junior partner. 'I wonder if I might have a further word with—'

'No time!' exclaimed Utterson. 'Out of my way, for the love of God!'

Threading his way among clerks and carts, Utterson arrived at Essex Street and demanded to see Rupert Kemp, whom he knew from the Law Society.

'Oh, I was close enough to Thomas Jekyll,' the leonine lawyer admitted a few minutes later, in the comfort of his wood-panelled office. 'I considered him a friend above all else, much as you did Henry. And, rather as in matters between you and Henry, I could not, in the end, prevent his fall. Why do you ask, though, Utterson? Is it something to do with the sudden return of his brother?'

Kemp was a most reliable man, as sharp as a rapier, and Utterson felt little hesitation in being as honest as possible.

'It's a complicated business,' he replied, mopping his brow. 'But lately I have been given to wonder if Jekyll's brother—your old friend Thomas—is in fact dead.'

Kemp smirked. 'My dear fellow, you're not suggesting that Thomas Jekyll might have taken his brother's place, in some bold attempt to claim his estate?'

Utterson grunted. 'It seems my suspicions have preceded me.'

'Well, there's been some talk in legal circles, as you might expect. But whatever your theory, I can put your mind at rest. For a start, Thomas looked only faintly like Henry—they were half-brothers, as you know—and as for his death, I can verify it categorically, for I was the one who was called in to identify him.'

'You saw him with your own eyes?'

'And smelled him with my nostrils. Moreover the parlous state of the body alone indicated that Thomas would never be rising from the dead.'

'Decayed?'

'And mutilated.'

'Was there no clue to the identity of the assailants?'

'Well, Thomas kept some questionable company, there's no doubt of that. I often feared for him, and quite justly as it turned out. But no,' said Kemp, 'there were no obvious culprits. And in any case the trail had gone completely cold by the time the body was discovered. Thomas had been due to travel to America, you see, and for a long time his absence was not regarded as suspicious.'

Utterson thought about it. 'Due to go to America, you say?'

'For weeks after his death everyone believed he was merely out of the country.'

'And does that itself not sound to you like the work of professionals?'

'What do you mean?'

'Well, to dispose of a man at the most advantageous time . . . when he is due to be abroad . . . when no one would suspect foul play until it was too late?'

'It's an intriguing possibility.'

Utterson thought some more. 'In fact, do you not think it possible that a well-prepared criminal—or even a team of them— might spend months, perhaps years, cobbling together the habits and history of a missing gentleman, with a view to assuming his identity at some stage?'

Kemp shrugged. 'It's an arresting notion,' he admitted, 'and not without precedent, I suppose.' He shook his head and chuckled. 'But really, Utterson, you have developed a devious mind in the past few years, haven't you?'

'Only in the past ten days,' Utterson replied. 'Only in the past ten days . . .'

He left Kemp's office with Richard Enfield's door key burning in his pocket. Though he had all but forgotten his kinsman in his mounting confusion, the mention of Thomas Jekyll's thwarted voyage to America had raised another terrible possibility. And so, fully prepared for the worst, he scaled the gloomy steps to Enfield's apartment in Piccadilly with his cane gripped tightly in his hand.

As soon as the door fell open he smelled the decay. Dead flowers, dead air, dead meat. He locked his throat and proceeded catlike through the rooms. It did not take long.

Richard Enfield was lying face down in the drawing room. There was a stain of long-dried blood extending from his head across the Turkey carpet. Travel bags and portmanteaus were piled nearby. A steamer trunk, monogrammed R.E., towered over the body like a headstone.

Kneeling down—blackbeetles scurried from the corpse—Utterson examined a huge depression, filled with maggots, in the side of his kinsman's head. The result of a heavy blow from a metal bar or hatchet, no doubt—enough to end Enfield's life in an instant. Killed, conceivably, because he could identify the mysterious man at his club. Killed, quite likely, because he was too close to Utterson. Killed, very possibly, because he was on the verge of revealing something incriminating.

But that he had been killed by the claimant or his hounds—that much, to Utterson, seemed beyond dispute.

For all that, he knew how the others would respond. A mere accident, they would say. Lamentable, no doubt, but much more common than one might think. *He tripped and struck his head on the corner of the table—look, you can even see some hair on the marble edge. And there, the bar of toilet soap upon which he slipped . . .*

And as for foul play, they would dismiss any suggestion of it at once. Unless of course they decided that Utterson himself—the only man in London with Enfield's door key—was responsible. *He had been acting very strangely, my lord, and clearly had many things to hide . . .*

In either case, they would be hellishly wrong.

Wouldn't they?

Utterson took off his hat and said a prayer for his last remaining friend. He recalled the many walks they had shared together, the vigorous debates in which they had engaged, and he vowed with all his heart to rain justice on the impostor and his piratical crew. Because this was no longer a mere personal grievance—it had a sacred purpose now.

Then, resisting the impulse to check for missing valuables, he backed out of Enfield's flat, made sure the stairway was deserted, and headed swiftly for the street, the brim of his hat pressed low on his head.

A Departing Soul

B Y MID-AFTERNOON, UNDER ragged black clouds, Utterson was at B— Municipal Cemetery, where he found the corpulent Irish groundskeeper frantically trying to conceal a flask.

'Seven years ago,' he told the groundskeeper tightly, 'I paid for the internment of a man called Edward Hyde. The man was a criminal—a murderer, in fact—yet I felt compelled to see him given a Christian burial owing to my particular friendship with his guardian, a doctor of some renown. However, I did not myself attend the burial, only paid for the headstone, so I have no idea where in this yard he is resting.'

'I know the grave well enough,' the groundskeeper said, wiping his lips with the back of his hand. 'A common plot—I can lead you there now.'

'There is more to it than that,' Utterson went on. 'You see, I would like to inspect the body.'

'*Inspect* it, sir?'

'In fact, I *demand* it. I want to see the body exhumed, as soon as possible.'

'*Today*, sir?'

'Right away. And I shall pay whatever is necessary.'

The groundskeeper shook his head. 'But that requires an order from—'

'No,' Utterson said firmly, 'it does not. I am a lawyer, sir, and I own the man's plot. The man has no remaining family whatsoever and I am his legal guardian. So I have a right to demand a disinterment.'

In fact, after leaving Enfield's apartment Utterson had been overwhelmed by the need to see Edward Hyde's body. He needed to verify, once and for all, that the little monster was really dead. Because, if he could do that, he might quell any remaining doubts that the wretched fellow had really been revived somehow, and Jekyll along with him.

'Maybe so,' the groundskeeper went on, 'but this is not my responsibility. I was not here seven years ago, and had nothing to do with his burial.'

'That is of no importance to me.'

'I was not here at the time,' the groundskeeper insisted. 'The feller here back then . . . he was discharged . . . the gravediggers, too . . . I was not here, I tell you.'

Utterson held up a placating hand. 'I am not here to investigate your practices, I assure you. I merely wish to see the body once in order to satisfy myself of its condition. So let us proceed without delay. Here'— he fished around in his pocket—'have a guinea now, in advance, for your trouble.'

No more than half an hour later they were in an ill-manicured corner of the cemetery thick with listing headstones and witch-chair grass. The gravediggers, humming music hall ditties, shovelled aside the sodden earth and exposed the rotting timbers of Hyde's coffin.

'Are you sure you know what to expect, Mr. Utterson?' the groundskeeper asked apprehensively. 'After seven years in a grave a body can change, I can tell you.'

'I shall recognise him, sir, have no doubt of that—from his frame alone.'

When the lid was prised open a gust of wind prickled through the yard, startling the blackbirds in the yew trees. A mist curled out like a departing soul. And everyone, Utterson included, tilted forward.

The gravediggers gasped. The groundskeeper made a rapid sign of the cross.

But Utterson, with a resilience that was becoming second nature, merely chuckled.

The coffin of Edward Hyde was empty.

Blasphemy of Blasphemies

T HE FELLER BEFORE me,' the groundskeeper mumbled, 'was a bad 'un. He robbed the dead of jewellery and stripped them of their clothes, and if there were no kinsmen he'd hawk the bodies too. It's by no means impossible that your friend Mr. Hyde did not even make it into his grave, or was dug out soon after. I am much aggrieved to tell you this, Mr. Utterson, and I hope it has not come as too much of a shock to you—but I say to you again, and I vouch for it on the grave of my own dear Ma, that this crime had nothing to do with me.'

Utterson, however, was not even listening. As a Christian, he attended church weekly, observed all the major feast days, read theology, and practised as well as he could the teachings of the testaments. So when the path of life twisted unexpectedly, or when he was forced to weather a storm or two, he armoured himself with the conviction that the vicissitudes of men's lives were designed to strengthen, not weaken, their pacts with God.

But now, with a blank smile fixed almost permanently on his face, he had begun to wonder if God were not so much testing as torturing him. If he had been singled out for punishment, if not death. If he had become the plaything of higher beings. And if—blasphemy of blasphemies—God and Satan had become one.

By the time he reached Gaunt Street the clerks were filing home from the counting houses. In the entrance hall Poole was waiting with the day's mail: a letter from Mr. Slaughter, which Utterson ignored; something from Dover—obsolete information relating to Enfield's whereabouts; and a third letter, written it seemed in some haste, from Mr. Kemp the solicitor.

Utterson was turning this envelope over in his hand when he noticed his butler standing beside him.

'You have something to say, Poole?'

Poole's cheeks coloured. 'It's about Dr. Jekyll, sir.'

'What about him?'

'Well, sir . . .' The butler shifted. 'The doctor has been in contact with me, you see, and—'

Utterson snorted. 'He has asked you to become his butler again, has he?'

'Well, sir—'

'And you wish to be released immediately into his service, is that it?'

'Well, I—'

Utterson shook his head. '*Et tu, Brute?*'

'Sir?'

'It matters not,' said Utterson. 'He has planned this, you know. Dr. Guise has planned everything. He thinks you have some knowledge he can plunder. Or he believes that your testimony will prove the most valuable endorsement of all. Whatever the case, he will use you, Poole, as he has used so many others before you, and then he will discard you.'

'Sir, I'm not sure—'

'No, he will discard you, I say. He will kill you. He will kill you and not even blink. And when that moment comes, Poole'—Utterson was staring into the butler's eyes—'when that moment comes, I want you to think of me, your former master, and I want you to breathe an apology to old Mr. Utterson. And then I want you to walk—no, *jump*—into the grave you have dug for yourself.'

Poole stiffened. 'If that is the way you feel—'

'Oh, get out of my sight, you stupid flunky! Pack your belongings and be off, damn you! A pox on you and all the men you have served—a pox on the lot of them!'

And without waiting for a response he stormed up to his business room, where he tore open Kemp's letter:

My dear Utterson—

Today you raised the possibility of an impostor, or a team of them, studying the life of a missing person with a view to inhabiting fraudulently the existence of said person.

I claimed that such a crime would not be without precedent, but it was only after you departed that I recalled a remarkably similar case, not ten years old, in Edinburgh. A man called Alexander MacKenzie, a prominent laird, had been presumed dead for close to seven years when a gentleman of strikingly similar appearance showed up in the city claiming to be the missing man. His bearing, his manners, his diction, his intimate knowledge of MacKenzie's habits and history, proved enough to convince even the most doubtful of men that he was indeed the wayward aristocrat. But just days after assuming full control of the estate he disappeared without a trace, taking the laird's considerable riches with him, and (to the extent that I am aware) there is no further knowledge of his whereabouts.

I trust this has been some help to you, without causing you further distress.

Sincerely yours,
RUPERT KEMP

Utterson feverishly packed a valise and headed downstairs, where he bumped into Poole, who was leaving with his own carpetbag. The two men said nothing to each other, not even a muttered oath, and at the corner went in entirely different directions—the butler to the house of his once and future master; the lawyer to King's Cross Station, and from there by the night train to Edinburgh.

A City In Disguise

I N THE MORNING, before the train had even squealed to a
halt, Utterson erupted onto the platform and shot up the
ramp to Waverley Bridge. He expected roiling clouds, exco-
riating winds, smoke vomiting from chimney stacks, the stink of
brewery waste and coal smoke—everything he knew from previous visits to Edinburgh. But the low-arching sun, stripped of
all veils, was gilding the gables of the Old Town, sparkling in
the shop windows of Princes Street, and flooding the crescents
of the New Town with bronze-flecked reflections. Whole cities,
it seemed, had costumed themselves in finery to rattle his mind.

Within minutes he was at the George Street address of The-
odore Macleod & Sons, a corresponding partner of Utterson &
Slaughter. Here he met Tarquin Macleod, a junior associate,
who admitted passing familiarity with the case of the 'MacKenzie claimant', while noting that the official legal adviser to the
laird (and for that matter his impersonator) was Mr. Carroll of
Shandwick Place. But since Mr. Carroll had 'gone soft in the
head', Utterson would be much better consulting Mr. Richard
Pringle of the *Edinburgh Evening News*—a man uniquely well-
versed in the city's criminal history.

Expecting another dour little Scot, granite of face and personality, Utterson was surprised to find in Pringle an energetic, flame-haired young fellow—thirty-five years at most—in gaily-coloured suspenders and ink-stained shirtsleeves.

'Aye, I remember the claimant well enough,' the man said, brewing tea. 'I was serving in the City Police at the time, working under an inspector by the name of Groves. I cannot tell you that the investigation was anything to be proud of—Groves, who took his own life last year, was not the brightest of men—but the facts of the case certainly made an impression on me, for I believe it was one of the boldest and yet most meticulous crimes this city has ever seen, and the claimant one of the boldest and yet most brilliant rogues ever to stalk these streets. Sugar?'

'I beg your pardon?'

'In your tea?'

'No, thank you. I mean yes, thank you. I mean—you were saying about the claimant?' Utterson, still clutching his valise, was leaning forward in his seat.

'The claimant, yes. He was a devilishly clever one, that's for sure. It's not just that he fooled Groves—no great accomplishment, it must be said—but that he duped some of MacKenzie's closest acquaintances, even his family members.'

'MacKenzie had relations?'

'Not many, and distant ones at that. He was something of a recluse, in fact, living alone on his estate at Kirkliston—precisely the reason, I suspect, that his identity was so easily fabricated when he disappeared.'

'And how exactly did he disappear?' asked Utterson.

'Well, that's always been something of a mystery. It's generally believed he came to grief on one of his hikes through the Highlands—that he fell down a mine shaft or some such thing—but no one can say for sure. Perhaps he ended his own life. Perhaps he was dispatched by some means or other. He was not expected to return, in any case, so there was a good deal of surprise when he did. I hope it's not too hot?' Pringle placed a steaming cup upon the table.

'Yes, thank you,' Utterson said, ignoring the tea completely. 'I mean, no thank you. I mean, who was in line to inherit the estate?'

'Some nieces and nephews from Boston, I believe. But alas, that was not to be, for the claimant successfully proved his identity—fraudulently, as we know now—and liquidated the riches before vanishing without a trace.'

'So the claimant thoroughly researched MacKenzie's life in advance, it's safe to say?'

'Most thoroughly. Comprehensively. Collecting information from friends, business associates, club members, even tradesman who had worked on the estate. Leaving no stone unturned. And all this so discreetly that nobody at the time was moved to suspicion.'

'And what about those who furnished this information—what happened to them?'

'Ah, you know about that as well, do you?'

Utterson squeezed his valise. 'Know what?'

Pringle, however, suddenly changed direction. 'May I ask, Mr. Utterson, if you knew Mr. MacKenzie personally? Or are you merely representing someone who did?'

Utterson straightened. 'I am representing someone in London who finds himself in a remarkably similar situation—someone due to inherit an estate that may yet be denied him, by a man who could very well be the same rogue who plied his trade here in Edinburgh.'

'You don't say?' Pringle stirred his own drink. 'The same impostor, you think, but claiming another estate?'

'A scoundrel whose methods seem identical to those you have described. A heartless murderer, not above eliminating those who know too much about him.'

'And robbing them at the same time?'

Utterson squinted. 'I beg your pardon?'

Pringle put down his spoon with a clink. 'Well, if we are speaking of the same man—and it would be most satisfying to think that we are—then you should know that part of the man's devilry was to case out the homes of MacKenzie's acquaintances, even while re-introducing himself to them, and later send in one of his accomplices, a one-time chimney sweep, to invade their homes through the roof.'

Utterson was chilled. 'A chimney sweeper?'

'That's right.'

'So the man had an accomplice?'

'He did.'

'Then tell me'—Utterson's voice snagged in his throat—'then tell me . . . was this chimney sweeper a swarthy little fellow with a particularly ugly visage?'

'He was indeed,' Pringle confirmed. 'Why? You have met the rascal yourself?'

Utterson began to shake. 'I might have done.'

'Then you can count yourself lucky that you are still alive, Mr. Utterson. The claimant and his accomplices stole a great deal of bounty from the homes of the unsuspecting, and did not hesitate to kill if they needed to. Though of course they did their best to disguise the crimes as natural accidents—fooling many, including the law here, I'm ashamed to say.'

'So perhaps,' Utterson said, swallowing, 'so perhaps a dead man might be found with a crack in his skull, and it would be mistakenly assumed that he struck his head against a bannister or a table?'

'That's it precisely. They were exceptionally proficient at covering their tracks. Even after making off with their loot they were at great pains to destroy all evidence. A young secretary at the claimant's law firm, for instance, had recorded details of his dealings with the men, on the instruction of the police, only to be found garrotted days later, with all his records missing.'

Utterson shuddered. 'And tell me,' he said, his voice lowering to a whisper, 'tell me, was this impostor, the man who took the place of MacKenzie . . . would you recall what he looked like?'

'I saw him myself on several occasions.'

'Then was he . . . was he . . .' Utterson moistened his lips. 'Was he an especially handsome, statuesque fellow with a Mediterranean pallor, and glossy brown eyes, and thick well-groomed hair, and sparkling white teeth?'

Pringle frowned. 'Why no . . . no . . . he was not like that at all.'

'No?'

'Not handsome at all, I'm afraid. Though neither was MacKenzie, the man he was impersonating.'

Utterson grasped at other possibilities. 'Then perhaps he was just in disguise . . . an elaborate disguise?'

'I doubt that any man could have disguised himself to that extent. For MacKenzie was broad and stocky, and very unprepossessing in looks.'

'Then perhaps . . .' Utterson began despairingly, but found he could not continue: *Then perhaps we are not speaking of the same man after all . . .*

'Please,' Pringle decided. 'Allow me a minute or two. The claimant never allowed himself to be photographed, it's true, but in the files here we have a portrait of Alexander MacKenzie, and that itself should give you a good idea of the claimant's appearance.'

Pringle made off to the newspaper's library as Utterson brooded over this strange turn of events. Were there two different impostors? Had he come to Edinburgh chasing shadows? Could God be mocking him one final time? The floor beneath his feet was vibrating with the thunder of the printing presses.

'Here it is,' said Pringle, returning with a folio sheet. 'An engraving of Alexander MacKenzie. Which, minus a few years perhaps, is identical to the appearance of the man who assumed his identity.'

Utterson looked down at the picture and immediately gasped.

The man in the portrait was the spitting image of Baxter, the bent-nosed butler!

He Knew What They Would Say

SITTING IN THE carriage of the train, armed with a sheaf of newspaper accounts and police reports as thick as a Bradshaw's, Utterson felt vindicated. He was not mad. He was not even eccentric. Indeed, it was darker and more sinister than anything he had imagined. The impostor and his associates had committed all manner of crimes in the past—fraud, theft, murder—and escaped without a single conviction. Small wonder, then, that they acted with such audacity now—because they fully expected to escape scot-free again!

Nonetheless Utterson had little confidence that any of his new evidence would convince Inspector Newcomen and his colleagues. The claimant had already done enough to discredit him fatally in their eyes. And he knew exactly what they would say.

The portrait of the MacKenzie claimant, for instance: they would insist that it bore only a faint resemblance to Butler. Or Baxter. Whatever he was called.. They would cite the unblemished nose, the flat ears, the more prominent chin. They would insist that the real MacKenzie looked considerably older than his supposed impersonator. And they would reject the very possibility that a gruffly mannered boxer could ever pass himself off as a Scottish laird.

They would sniff indifferently at the newspaper descriptions of the MacKenzie claimant's manservant (Spanish, dark-haired, meticulously groomed), denying that they proved, as Utterson firmly believed, that this was the man presently masquerading as Henry Jekyll.

They would argue, too, that the MacKenzie claimant's errand boy—the former chimney sweeper—was clearly not the same person as the Jekyll claimant's knife-boy Eddie. To do so they would make the most of the differences apparent in the police report—where the chimney sweeper was broadly described as 'Mongoloid' and 'simian'—before declaring that the two were entirely different men.

They would delight in pointing out that the man claiming to be Jekyll had amassed an impressive number of affidavits from men of rank, wilfully ignoring all the affidavits the MacKenzie claimant had similarly accrued—as if the endorsements of London gentlemen were plainly more credible than those of whisky-bibbing Scotsmen!

And finally they would say that Utterson had already proved himself to be entirely unreliable. They would recall his false accusations and preposterous theories. They would sneer at his absurd insistence that Jekyll and Hyde were the same man. They would murmur about the vast inheritance of which he stood to be deprived. They would encourage Poole to recount details of his erratic behaviour. They would chuckle about his unrequited love for the widow Spratling. They might even have learned of his desperate assault on the impostor and the widow in a West End alley . . . *no, wait*, Utterson thought, *that was only a dream . . .*

In any event, it was enough to know that there had been other victims before him, and now, if nothing else, he could at least prevent the same fate befalling others in the future. But how, exactly, would he confront the villains? What could he, a lean lawyer in his late fifties, hope to accomplish against a ruthless gang of three? Should he threaten them? Abduct them? Was he ready, God forbid, to sacrifice his own life? Or were the impostors intending to do away with him right now—with just one day remaining before Jekyll was to be declared officially dead?

Such were the questions that swirled through Utterson's mind as the train streaked through the quilted English countryside and the necklace of noble cities between Edinburgh and London.

He shot out of King's Cross glancing repeatedly over his shoulder. He dived into a cab and rattled home with his heart thumping. He dashed for the door and was fumbling for his key—there was no longer any butler to open the place—when a figure emerged from the shadows next door. Utterson drew back defensively, raising his owl-headed cane.

But it was only his neighbour, the retired surveyor Mr. Grimsby. 'The postman asked me to pass this over,' Grimsby explained, handing across some mail and frowning concernedly. 'But is something ailing you, Mr. Utterson? You look unwell.'

'Unwell?' Utterson laughed. 'I've never been better!'

In the hall he made a cursory examination of the letters, flinging aside two messages from Mr. Slaughter before tearing open a parcel from the chemist Enoch Fell.

Inside was a fold of coloured paper with an explanatory note:

SIR—

I have been told that you have been searching for a special Provision of Salt, of a Type that was supplied by me to HENRY JEKYLL. The Salt was from a Consignment that I purchased from a disreputable Dealer in CHEAPSIDE, my usual Dealer being absent.

I later learned that this Salt had been stored in a Vessel also containing various other Salts, in sufficient quantities to contaminate the marked Powder. I thereafter refrained from selling this Salt, but retained a small Quantity lest it be required again.

I herewith enclose a measure of this Salt, in the hope that it proves useful to you, but under the circumstances I have decided not to include a Bill. I trust you to use this Substance judiciously.

Your faithful Servant,
Enoch Fell, CHEMIST

Utterson shivered. As much as he had felt as if higher powers were mocking him, he now wondered if God Himself might not be guiding him down the final path. For here, on top of all the evidence he had amassed in Edinburgh, was the last piece of the puzzle—the powder that made the potion complete. And here, too, was the answer to all his problems: a means of disguising himself and gaining inhuman strength in the process. He would confront the villains now, he would overpower them, and he would escape without ever being identified.

The bell tinkled on the porch. Utterson raised his cane and tore open the door, ready for anything. But it was only his head clerk.

'Mr. Utterson,' said Guest, doffing his hat, 'may I have a word?'

Utterson was on the point of slamming the door before realising that this was exactly what he required. 'By all means!' he declared, practically dragging the young man inside. 'Come in, dear Guest, and observe!'

In the hallway Guest attempted to splutter something but Utterson had no time for it.

'Never mind that!' he said. 'You are here for a reason, did you know that? You have been sent by God! You are a holy chronicler. *You have a divine purpose!*'

He shoved the clerk up the stairs to his business room, where he frantically added Fell's salt to the other ingredients and stirred them furiously in a glass while informing Guest of everything he had discovered in Edinburgh—the full story of the MacKenzie claimant and everything before that.

'So beware, dear fellow, for your own life!' he finished. 'Beware, at all times, of Dr. Guise!'

'Sir, sir'—Guest looked confounded—'you're not going to *drink* that liquid?'

'Oh, do not concern yourself for me—do not worry for a minute about Gabriel Utterson—*for just as Satan transformed into an angel of light, so an angel of light will now transform into Satan!*'

And with that he seized the glass of foaming liquid and hurled it down his throat, slamming the empty glass back onto the table and wiping his lips with the back of his sleeve.

Then he stared at Guest even as his vision blurred and swam and his muscles throbbed and fluttered, as his blood heated and stormed through his head, as his muscles swelled and rearranged; his bones contorted audibly, his hair twisted, his teeth and nails lengthened, his back arched; and he saw the look of astonishment—of sheer disbelief—on his head clerk's face.

But no, this was no dream—Utterson knew it this time. *This was reality*. This was actually happening. Foundations were crumbling, walls were collapsing; he had finally done it. He had breached—no, *demolished*—the fortress of identity.

Teddy Guest's Statement of the Case

I T IS NOW over twenty-four hours since the events of yesterday evening and it has become my unhappy task to put on
paper my thoughts regarding Mr. Gabriel Utterson and the
madness that ultimately claimed him. Detective Inspector Newcomen of Scotland Yard has promised to visit me shortly, both to
collect my statement and to inspect some other documents in my
possession, so there is no certainty that I shall be able to complete this narrative in time for his perusal. Nevertheless, as much
as my hand trembles as I write this, I regard it as something of a
sacred duty—'a holy purpose' as Mr. Utterson himself might
have called it—to record these recollections for posterity, and to
leave others to make of it what they will.

I first came into contact with Mr. Utterson some fourteen
years ago, shortly after he entered into partnership with Mr.
Slaughter, and not long before the two men moved into the
premises in Bedford Row (which the firm still occupies). Owing
to the straitened circumstances of my employer at that stage, and
the high regard in which my penmanship was held—for I believe
I can say without hubris that I was among the best of my profession, mentioned in the same breath as Mr. Greaves of Burton &
Leach and Mr. Fairley of Marshall, Bidwell & Swanston—I

quickly found myself transferred to the front desk of Utterson & Slaughter, a post which I quickly made my domicile.

I must say now without hesitation that I am forever indebted to Mr. Utterson; both for employing me in the first place and thereafter for championing me at every opportunity. He became, *in loco parentis*, a fatherly figure to me, most keenly interested in my progress and unflaggingly helpful in matters both professional and personal. He never intimidated me, never admonished me publicly, and was always quick to acknowledge my good work and punctuality. A most ascetic man in all but his weakness for vintage wines, he even extended to me the intimacy of his own home on some occasions (the greatest honour of which I believe he was capable), and rarely hesitated to entrust me with the knowledge of all his doubts and uncertainties (of which, before his decline, there were conspicuously few).

He also proved peerlessly supportive and understanding when I was forced to take my dear father, a former bookkeeper from Tavistock, into my meagre lodgings in London. My father's faculties by this stage had so failed that the task of caring for him occupied my every free hour, and often necessitated my absence from Bedford Row for long periods. Yet even when some in the firm questioned my priorities, and when Mr. Slaughter agitated for some redress, Mr. Utterson was my most resolute guardian and defender. He would not hear of any penalty, neither in salary nor status, and when my father eventually passed on to a better life, Mr. Utterson's first impulse was to console me like an uncle, to share my grief, and to welcome my return to the office with all the privileges to which I had become accustomed.

Nonetheless, it was through supporting my father in his final years that I became, for better and worse, something of an expert in the frailty of the human condition and the fine lines that separate the strong-minded from the eccentric and the eccentric from the outright mad. It was indeed a terrible thing to witness my father, a man who had been a fund of common sense and practical facts, disintegrate to the point where he was incapable of remembering his activities of minutes previously, was confused as to his own whereabouts, suspicious of others' intentions, and at a loss to nominate the most important people and events of his life. Incrementally, and yet right before my eyes, a proud man had been shorn of his dignity, indeed his very identity.

In the case of Mr. Utterson, I am inclined to believe that his disintegration, more sudden than incremental (and confined therein to two unexpected surges), commenced about seven years ago amid the mysterious circumstances surrounding the disappearance of his good friend Dr. Henry Jekyll. To that point the closest Mr. Utterson had come to 'eccentric behaviour' was through his curious collection of walking sticks, for not a month seemed to pass without his purchasing of a new cane, frequently capped with an animal head, which he would flourish ostentatiously around the office as if to invite admiration. Why he found it necessary to own such a forest of sticks, and what he did with them once they were no longer required, has always been something of a mystery to those of us in the office; but I have always suspected that Mr. Utterson, when still a youth, must have fixed his mind on owning such objects, and endowed them with great symbolic importance, to the extent that all his success never exhausted his need to assert his status, or gain for himself some notional security, through the purchase of a new cane.

Except for this endearing idiosyncrasy, I believe I can say that I have never met a man less whimsical in outlook than Mr. Gabriel Utterson. It was indeed this quality that made him such a model of sanity for all in his circle. He was keenly aware of this—he conceded as much to me openly—and had made something of a plaque of it, for he was justifiably proud of his status as 'a lighthouse around which other vessels flounder and occasionally wreck'.

Certainly one of those vessels was Henry Jekyll. Of the doctor's activities immediately preceding his disappearance I know very little, except to say that they were most uncharacteristic. In my dealings with him to that point, through his patronage of the law firm, I had always found him to be a character of exceptional good sense and generosity. This was a man who would pay a bill without even studying it, would never quibble about trivial matters, and would always be ready for a cheerful conversation about subjects far and wide. He was an alchemist as much as a physician, with a great interest in formulating medicines with which he hoped to combat all sorts of maladies, and to this mission he committed himself with a fakir's devotion. As for Mr. Hyde, I never met him personally, only heard about him through gossip, but like many others I am given to believe that this disagreeable little man, whatever his background, was merely a volunteer who agreed to partake of the doctor's elixirs and submit to his subsequent examinations for a negotiated payment. He may indeed have had some malign influence on Jekyll, or it could be that the doctor was troubled by the failure of his experiments; whatever the case, there is little doubt that, before his disappearance, Dr.

Jekyll became unusually distracted, exhibiting a nature that swung wildly between deep despondence and wild exuberance.

Mr. Utterson clearly blamed Hyde for this disequilibrium and cultivated many sinister theories about him. I myself may have unwittingly encouraged such notions when I was called upon to examine a letter written in Hyde's hand, whereupon I noted the script's similarity to that of Dr. Jekyll; and from this innocent observation Mr. Utterson concluded for some reason that Jekyll was *forging* letters for Hyde (before reaching, it has only recently become evident, an even more fantastical conclusion).

That Mr. Hyde was a murderer there can be little doubt, and that Jekyll gave him refuge, perhaps as a result of his own complicity, also seems possible. Whatever the truth of their relationship, it is certain that Mr. Utterson was deeply unsettled by it, having appointed himself as Jekyll's keeper if not his guardian angel. Determined therefore to prise the two men apart, he nightly prowled the streets around the Jekyll home, and pursued Mr. Hyde like a hound, and was so dazzled by the spell of this self-appointed mission that he lost sight, for the first time in his life, of his professional responsibilities.

(It should be noted in passing that the walking stick used by Mr. Hyde to murder Sir Danvers Carew had earlier been a gift to Dr. Jekyll by Mr. Utterson, so it is not inconceivable that the very idea that one of his canes had been so inconsiderately passed on to another man, and a common criminal at that, was enough to ignite in Mr. Utterson a great deal of self-destructive umbrage and jealousy.)

In any event, it was around this time that we in the office noticed Mr. Utterson's unexplained absences, his occasionally dishevelled appearance, his unwonted shortness of temper, his general impatience with quotidian matters, along with his occasional lapses of memory. But we took these to be temporary afflictions, with no enduring consequences—failing to see in them the first flickers of a madness that would ultimately overwhelm him.

Certainly the suicide of Mr. Hyde, together with the disappearance of Dr. Jekyll, brought the more obvious symptoms temporarily to an end, for Mr. Utterson returned to the office and attended to his clients with the dedication for which he was famous. Only those of us who were closest to him recognised a mysterious new cast to his personality, something between that of a man who had survived a great trauma and a treasure hunter after discovering a pirate's cave.

It is to be admitted here that few of us thought well of this change. In fact, there was considerable disquiet within the firm about some lingering mysteries. Why, for instance, had Jekyll suddenly named Mr. Utterson as his sole beneficiary shortly before his disappearance? And why did Mr. Utterson seem so unconcerned about his friend's fate (almost as though he knew that the doctor would never return)? Rumours flourished for a while, always behind Mr. Utterson's back, and may have sent forth shoots in many preposterous directions; it is enough to say that a general suspicion thereafter hung over Mr. Utterson, and caused many to deal with him with studied reserve.

But after a while no more was said about the matter, and the weeds of suspicion without nourishment failed to thrive, and for my part I was too occupied with caring for my father to be exercised by such dark notions.

Approaching the seventh anniversary of the doctor's disappearance, however, few in the office could not but notice a renewed disturbance in Mr. Utterson. For suddenly this man of flinty asceticism was muttering whimsical philosophies, staring into middle-space for long periods, and rushing away at the day's end with little concern for his unfinished work. Not only, it seemed, was he speculating about what he would do with his forthcoming riches, but he suddenly had romantic aspirations as well—for he had been spotted around town with a matronly woman, an ostentatious widow said to have 'a special regard' for newly prosperous men.

Now as much as Jekyll's relationship with Mr. Hyde was the cause of much consternation to Mr. Utterson, so this unexpected *affaire de cœur* proved deeply unsettling to me. For I had long regarded Mr. Utterson as a personal hero, who had forged a path that I was destined to follow; and much of what I found so admirable in the man was his determination to spurn those matters which can so weaken one's resolve—by which I mean the reading of unedifying novels, the patronage of the meretricious arts and the courting of facile ladies. For most of the time I knew him Mr. Utterson seemed merrily immune to such fancies, with no appreciable debit from his wellbeing—indeed, he seemed proof that one could prosper in life without polluting one's heart with romantic love.

'The measure of a man's unhappiness is the distance between where he is and where he aspires to be.' This pearl of wisdom, which so impressed me that I recorded it in my day-book, and muttered it like a biblical verse thereafter, was offered to me by Mr. Utterson himself in the days when happiness and unhappiness seemed to him as indistinguishable as flowers in a distant meadow.

And now this man with no time for dreams seemed so stricken with foolish fancies that I could only wonder what damage was being wrought on his mind. A person's identity (as I discovered with my father) is a fragile abode, pinned together with memories, beliefs, precepts, and perceptions of the self gleaned through the responses of others. But in Mr. Utterson's case this abode was a veritable palace, with towers, chambers and dungeons built on marble buttresses and huge oaken beams. And now this man, of all men, was trying to replace his palace with a castle in the air: a chimera, a phantom self, a dream of what he wanted to be!

It is precisely in such chasms that insanity breeds.

Now it would be unjust of me, of course, to claim that such dreams alone drove Mr. Utterson mad; but I knew enough to recognise a man who was no longer in complete control of his mind. And once again, together with the others in the firm, I saw in Mr. Utterson a confusion of purpose and dereliction of duty, along with a notable change of personal appearance (sometimes neglectful, sometimes incongruously overdressed).

Still nothing was said openly, and no sentiments shared beyond a few disapproving glances; and if some of our more discriminating clients were quietly steered in the direction of Mr. Slaughter, it was more through tacit agreement than official policy.

Things came to a head, however, with the unforeseen reappearance of Dr. Jekyll just two weeks ago. It suddenly became clear that Mr. Utterson had genuinely believed that Jekyll was dead (and not just missing); and so it was that the Jekyll claimant—who seemed authentic to all those who met him, and whose explanation for his absence proved highly credible—became in Mr. Utterson's eyes an ungodly charlatan, a thief of Jekyll's identity, who needed to be unmasked before he got his demonic hands on the doctor's fortune.

Suffice to say that Mr. Utterson's erratic behaviour very rapidly took on a darker hue. He was demonstrably agitated at work, with a temper that verged at times on the violent; he was intolerably rude to the company's clients; he was particularly abrasive with Mr. Slaughter; and he was unusually high-handed with the rest of the staff. He was waxen in complexion and lank of cheek; his fingernails were chewed to the quick; his hair resembled a fringe of ruffled feathers; his clothes were stained with wine; and meanwhile he jumbled names, forgot the most basic details, and to all appearances regarded his professional duties as a hindrance to more important pursuits. At one point he asked me to examine two examples of handwriting, convinced against all evidence that 'the impostor' was forging the real doctor's hand; at another he presented me with two weighty documents, charging me with the responsibility of concealing them lest he be killed or go missing; and on another occasion—the last time we saw him at Bedford Row—he muttered incomprehensible oaths before accosting Mr. Slaughter in the stairwell.

At about the same time we were visited by Inspector Newcomen of Scotland Yard, who revealed that Mr. Utterson was well known within the ranks of the police for prowling the area around Dr. Jekyll's home, day and night, to the point that it had become something of a sport for the local constables to sneak up on him and engage him in harmless conversation, just to find out what was on his mind. But Newcomen was reluctant to take action owing to Mr. Utterson's high standing around the Courts, though he admitted to having harboured concerns about the man's faculties for some time.

So Mr. Slaughter convened a meeting in the office and encouraged the staff to divulge all their concerns; and like wild horses that have been too long confined to a stable the employees revelled in their freedom. It is fair to say that the portrait that emerged of Mr. Utterson was that of a man whose temperament was a flimsy façade for a deeply troubled soul. With much regret, then, Mr. Slaughter resolved to ask Mr. Utterson to step down for a few months, at the end of which time a decision would be made regarding his future.

Mr. Slaughter intended to confront Mr. Utterson on the matter *in propria persona* but when the latter did not reappear that afternoon, or on the following day, numerous letters were dispatched to his Gaunt Street address, all without response. So I was charged with the responsibility of visiting Mr. Utterson in order to deliver a signed statement informing him of the company's resolution, and to wait for a suitable reply should Mr. Utterson choose not to return to the offices himself.

Upon my arrival, however, I found Mr. Utterson in such a state of feverish excitement that he would not listen to me. Rejecting all my efforts to make myself heard, he dragged me through the house and forced me to hear his mad diatribe.

He had just returned from Scotland, he claimed, where he had unearthed evidence that the Jekyll claimant had been involved in many sensational crimes, including murder. He warned that I myself was far from safe, as 'the demon' might arrive at my rooms at any time to strangle me.

He went on to recount the substance of the secret letters he had previously put in my custody—not to save me the trouble of reading them, he said, but simply to help explain what he was about to do. (For the record, I have since gone through these documents, which I have beside me now pending Inspector Newcomen's examination, and I am satisfied that they are bald fabrications. While purporting to be recreations of letters penned by Henry Jekyll and Hastie Lanyon, the narratives are so festooned with expressions I know to be idiomatic to Mr. Utterson—'the provinces of good and ill', 'a furious propensity to ill', 'the fortress of identity'—that I have little hesitation in identifying Mr. Utterson himself as their author.)

In any case, he claimed that Dr. Jekyll had concocted a magical drink that somehow converted him, like some character in a fairy tale, into Mr. Hyde. He admitted that he had been unable to prove this at first, owing to the absence of a special powder; but now that this powder had arrived—just minutes before my arrival, he claimed—the experiment could proceed with myself as witness.

'Behold!' he exclaimed. 'I am Satan!'—before drinking the bubbling potion.

Still I tried my utmost to stop him, but he forced me back into a chair where, dumbstruck, I watched as the formula took its effect. I saw his face contort, and his eyes roll back into his head; and his hands went to his throat, he gasped and wheezed; his body twisted; and for a few moments I almost believed that I was indeed watching a preternatural transformation.

But when he fell to his knees and began foaming at the mouth, I knew I was witnessing the convulsions of one poisoned, as I had seen the very same reaction in a man who had inadvertently swallowed rat bait in Tavistock (the man died shortly thereafter).

So I rushed from the house and thumped on all the neighbouring doors; finally I was able to locate a doctor and we made at great haste back to the Utterson abode. Alas, we had only made it to the threshold when a figure smashed between us and shot out into the street.

Though at first I feared it was an opportunistic thief who had taken advantage of the open door, it soon became clear that the figure was Mr. Utterson himself, possessed of some maniacal strength. By the time we had reclaimed our wits and set off in pursuit, he had already reached the corner and was heading for the City.

Quickly the doctor and I hailed a cab and gave chase, gaining ground just as he reached Waterloo Bridge. Now it must be admitted here that, for a man of his years, Mr. Utterson was moving with remarkable agility, capering like a monkey, springing over obstacles, bouncing off walls like a frenzied fly. And yet I had witnessed this phenomenon before, too, in the inmates of the Tavistock asylum, who once escaped and ran riot through the town, many of them performing astonishing feats of short-lived strength.

The streets by this time of night were largely empty, thank God, for I can only imagine what damage Mr. Utterson might have inflicted had his path been blocked. Even as it was, when I reached out from the cab to seize him, he turned on me with his eyes flaring and his mouth a rictus of yellowed teeth, and blasted at me a rank breath, and violently chopped my arm, before gal-loping down an unlit alley and away.

It was at this point that we lost him completely in a maze of streets, and we might have retired, or at least recruited assistance from a police station, but then an idea, or rather a certainty, took hold of me, which I conveyed at once to the driver of the cab.

For there could be only one place, in light of his obsession, to which Mr. Utterson could be heading—and that was to the home of Dr. Henry Jekyll.

My heart was crashing as we shot through the labyrinth, hoping desperately we would not be too late (for I have always admired the doctor, and was loath to see him attacked, let alone killed).

Alas, when we arrived at Jekyll's street it was to the sound of an unearthly squeal, half-human and half-bestial. The door to the doctor's home was flung wide and residents had gathered outside. I heard a frantic commotion, followed by a sickening whack, and when I looked up to the first-floor window (I swear to God) I saw a spray of blood blast across the window sashes, sending a lurid glow across the spectators below. And it was my gravest fear now that Mr. Utterson had already visited upon his nemesis the ultimate revenge.

I bounded up the stairs to the study and took in the ghastly tableau of four men splattered with blood and bodily matter. One was the stocky man I now know to be Baxter, sporting on his forehead a red mark (where, I later learned, Mr. Utterson had belted him with his cane); the second was Dr. Jekyll, who had collapsed onto an armchair with his hand over his heart; the third was Poole, standing in the middle of the room wielding in his hands a bloody axe; and lastly there was Mr. Utterson himself, twisted grotesquely on the floor.

The state of his body, in particular the damage inflicted—for there was a divot in his chest the size of an axe-head—indicated immediately that the life of the unhappy Mr. Gabriel Utterson had come to an end.

Still I struggled to accept it, for as much as I had lost all faith in my employer, I had never seriously contemplated his passing. There was, moreover, the dreadful expression on his face that I knew would haunt me long afterwards—a chilling look of fury and pain, beyond all powers of description.

For a while we all stood dumbstruck in that room, and if anyone said a word I was not in a state to hear it; and then, coming to my senses, I discovered that others had flooded in, among them officers of the police; and there was a whirl of movement as Utterson's body was covered with a shroud and others blotted blood from their clothes; and we were all transported somehow—I do not even remember how—to a police station, where we sat together awaiting questioning.

And it was here that Dr. Jekyll conversed with me for the first time in years. His voice croaked and his lips quivered as he spoke, but he was as sympathetic as he had ever been, remembering my name, even enquiring about my father, and apologising profusely for his part in drawing me into this terrible drama. He admitted that, as shocked as he was to find Utterson capable of such violent passions (not to mention such feats of twisted imagination), he had in his Cambridge days known a very different fellow—a 'high spirited boy' who was demonstrative, pugnacious, adventurous and greatly fond of pranks and whimsies. He said that the transformation, when it came, was as sudden as it was comprehensive; and though it was difficult to assign to it a single explanation, he suspected it had something to do with a romantic misadventure and a horrific night in a graveyard (neither of which he cared to discuss in any detail). It was clear, in any event, that this 'boisterous' Utterson had been lying dormant beneath the lawyer's leathery hide for years, needing only the shock of an unexpected development to regain command; and Jekyll's greatest regret now, he said, was that he had not diagnosed the extent of his friend's illness while he was still in a position to rescue him.

And I was tremendously moved by all this, and if I had any doubts about the doctor's identity they evaporated completely. For I could see that he spoke sincerely, with a tear glistening in his eye, and I further recognised in his noble face an integrity that I knew to be the stamp of trustworthy men. So, even in my shaken state, I was able to assure him that Utterson's mysterious 'transitions of personality' had troubled us for some time; and I went on to inform him of the man's absurd theories, his impulsive trip to Edinburgh, and even the fanciful letters he had left in my possession—letters that proved of such interest to Jekyll that he asked if he might examine them in person, before I should submit them to the police, in order to satisfy his medical interest.

'What feverish children we become when our dreams are disrupted,' he said—a sad epitaph, I thought, but no less accurate; and again I could not help but feel great pity for the man, that when he should have been celebrating his return he was instead deep in mourning (not just for Mr. Utterson, his most faithful friend, but for others in his circle who by unhappy chance had also gone to God shortly after welcoming him home).

Inspector Newcomen, too, was deeply perturbed when he questioned me, for while he had observed Mr. Utterson's descent into madness from the start, he admitted that he could not fully account for it, and had always held out hopes for the lawyer's recovery. So he urged me to write down everything I remembered as soon as I felt able—for, as he said, 'There are still many questions that need to be answered.'

Last night I was unable to sleep; and today I was given leave by Mr. Slaughter to collect my thoughts; and I spent much time walking the streets of London, beneath a sun so exuberant that the beasts in the city's menageries were trumpeting and hooting festively; and occasionally a tear wetted my cheek; and finally, when my hands had ceased trembling, I turned home.

And now, deep into the evening, as I prepare to lay down my pen, I see through the window a darkly caped gentleman alight from a cab outside my door—Dr. Jekyll, I believe, though it is difficult to be certain through the fog. But I cannot conclude this statement without observing, with deep sadness, that while we live in an age of unprecedented advancement, of steamships, locomotives and electric clocks, and of explorers penetrating heretofore unmapped regions of the world, the greatest mysteries, and indeed the greatest perils, remain hidden within the dungeons of the human imagination. For while our minds are unquestionably capable of wondrous and profound things, they also harbour a weakness for envy, jealousy, misapprehension, delusion, sensation, rationalisation, credulousness, outlandish whimsies, for distorting the motives of friends and attributing to others the powers of the devil—all of which I witnessed at firsthand during the strange case of Dr. Jekyll and Mr. Utterson.

Acknowledgments

Ariel Moy; Carl Harrison-Ford; Stephen Clarke; Holly Roberts; Rod Morrison and Roy Chen at Xoum; Campbell Brown, Alison McBride and Megan Duff at Black & White; and David Forrer at Inkwell.